HEARTACHE I

Harley Street is a world apart, full of tragedy, apprehension, relief and happiness. Heartache too, Nurse Anita Fielding discovers when she comes to work for consultant gynaecologist Ross Wyndham, who is not only a brilliant surgeon but also a charming and attractive man.

HEARTACHE IN
HARLEY STREET

BY

SONIA DEANE

MILLS & BOON LIMITED
London · Sydney · Toronto

First published in Great Britain 1984
by Mills & Boon Limited, 15–16 Brook's Mews,
London W1A 1DR

© Sonia Deane 1984

Australian copyright 1984
Philippine copyright 1984

ISBN 0 263 74686 0

Set in 11 on 12 pt Linotron Times
03–0584–48,450

Photoset by Rowland Phototypesetting Ltd
Bury St Edmunds, Suffolk
Made and printed in Great Britain by
Richard Clay (The Chaucer Press) Ltd
Bungay, Suffolk

CHAPTER ONE

Nurse Anita Fielding thought rebelliously that she had been mad to take a job with the eminent consultant gynaecologist, Ross Wyndham, when she had her SRN and the world could have been her oyster. But, she argued, the lure of Harley Street and a new adventure had been stronger than common sense. Now, here she was, ministering to the great man's professional needs and soothing anxious patients. She doubted, even so, if he would recognise her in the street, despite the fact that she had been with him a month.

As if to confound her theories, he looked up from his desk and said disarmingly, 'I'm still mystified by your coming to work here when you had so many other options open to you.'

Anita stared at him, amazed. She supposed he would be termed a handsome man, with strong, yet sensitive, features, level brows, and eyes that could be both fiery and sympathetic as the mood dictated. His face lit up when he smiled, and humour flashed unexpectedly.

'I'm a little baffled myself,' she admitted frankly. 'I think it was a question of curiosity and awe.'

'"Awe"?' he echoed, surprised, studying her as he spoke, liking her fearless eyes which were large and lustrous; passion hinted at, rather than boldly proclaimed. Her cap sat jauntily on her upswept shining dark hair, and the allure of her uniform seemed greater than the appeal of *haute couture*.

'Well,' she admitted, 'in hospital we are all alerted when consultants go on their rounds— students trailing behind them like a gaggle of geese!' She stopped half-apologetically, giving a little nervous laugh.

But his smile broadened and a deep-throated chuckle escaped him. 'I like the geese!' he said.

Anita hastened, 'The individual gets lost in the procession; one never has more than a glimpse of the actual man. I wanted a peep behind the scenes.'

Their eyes met in a sudden awareness of each other.

'And now?' He toyed with a paper-knife which he rocked up and down on his immaculate blotting-pad, continuing to hold her gaze.

'Everything seems just as hectic and impersonal . . . That's not quite what I mean, but there's even less time—' she smiled beguilingly—'and you, like all the others, are always late!'

He sighed, nodded, and said almost humbly, 'I *try* not to be. This is the first opportunity I've had really to talk to you,' he commented ruefully. 'And now only because of a cancellation.'

The atmosphere of the room changed miraculously, as though shadow had turned to dazzling light. It was a large lofty room, elegantly proportioned and furnished, which Anita had previously regarded as unfriendly, but which now appeared suddenly to have come to life.

'You are due at St Mark's at five-thirty,' she reminded him.

He glanced at his watch although a clock stared at him from his desk.

'I've only these letters to sign.' He indicated a pile on the blotting-pad. 'What part of the country do you come from? Oh, I know you have a flat near here but—'

'My familys' roots are in Sussex—near Horsham. I was born there. My father lost all his money when I was ten; the shock killed my mother and soon afterwards my father died too. I was shuttled from relative to relative, but I learned a good deal about life and people,' she added philosophically. 'And I always wanted to be a nurse . . .' She stopped abruptly, telling herself that she was talking too much.

'I'm glad you became one,' he said meaningly.

Excitement surged over her. His voice was low and intimate. Was it possible that this was Ross Wyndham with whom she had worked for a month?—pleasantly enough, she admitted, but as though they functioned in different worlds.

'I'm sorry about your parents.' He got up from his chair as he spoke, his tall lithe figure impressive. His dark suit, although formal, managed to appear casual because of the air with which he wore it. 'And glad that we've had these few words . . . You didn't come here at a particularly auspicious time,' he added.

Anita was baffled. 'In what way?'

'My ward is normally part of the practice. She takes care of reception and many other things . . . I expect Mrs Baxter (his secretary), or her assistant, will have told you.' He looked at Anita very levelly.

'Mrs Baxter has mentioned a Glynis Morgan who is on holiday, but that is all.' Actually Anita had found Mrs Baxter and her assistant, Emily, rather stand-offish and uncommunicative, but they had invested Glynis Morgan's name with importance.

'Glynis is my ward.' Ross Wyndham's expression was indulgent. 'You and she will have the loss of parents in common, since hers were killed in an air crash when she was fifteen, leaving her in my care. They were great friends of mine . . . You look startled. I suppose the word "ward" has an old-fashioned ring. Or does it make me sound ancient?'

'That is the last thing!' Anita protested. Studying him, she could not imagine a more virile, alert man. He was no more than thirty-two or three, she decided, feeling that there were, however, facets of his character which would always be subtly concealed. Thus, he became not only a challenge, but faintly mysterious. A strange uneasy sensation rushed upon her. In romantic novels the guardian always fell in love with his ward. What would Glynis be like? A feeling of disappointment crashed into a former eagerness as Anita contemplated the situation. Having talked to Ross Wyndham and brushed the edge of familiarity, she craved to know him better.

He returned to his desk. 'Glynis has been with friends on a winter cruise,' he explained easily. 'Now that spring is here—' he flicked his fountain pen from his waistcoat pocket—'she is ready to return home and to work.'

Where, Anita asked herself, was *home*? Did she live with Ross Wyndham in this house, which he owned and in which he had a flat? It struck her as unlikely. Mrs Baxter had volunteered the information about the house and flat, also that he had a housekeeper named Mrs Smithers.

Anita's puzzlement must have betrayed itself, for he added, 'Glynis lives with my stepmother in Devonshire Place. My parents were divorced,' he added swiftly. 'My mother also re-married, but my father unfortunately died of a coronary two years ago. My stepmother, Janet, and I are great friends . . . you must meet her sometime . . . Now to these letters, or Mrs Baxter will be chasing me.' He started putting his signature to them as he spoke. 'I don't know when I was last able to do this with a degree of leisure,' he added.

'Not since I've been here,' Anita said emphatically.

'It will probably be another month before it happens again!' He glanced up and met her somewhat astonished gaze. 'You didn't think I'd remember how long you've been with me—did you?'

'No,' she admitted, flushing slightly.

He lowered his gaze to his task again as he commented, 'I may not appear to notice what goes on around me, Nurse Fielding, but very little escapes me.'

Mrs Baxter rang on the inter-com. Could Emily collect the post?

Emily appeared a few seconds later. A plump girl in her early twenties, dominated by Mrs Baxter who was one of the old school, believing in discipline. Her office was the holy of holies and she would have known had anyone breathed on her typewriter which was sacrosanct. She was highly efficient and trustworthy, an old fifty-five. In fact it was impossible to believe that she had ever been young. Anita rightly felt that she, herself, posed a problem for Mrs Baxter who would have preferred a staid, humourless character whom she could also have moulded to her ways.

As Emily shut the door behind her, Ross Wyndham asked, 'Do you live alone?'

'Yes; I've tried sharing . . . the flat's mine. The one thing I own. A long-lost uncle left it to me. It's in Hill Mews; very small, but *mine*. You might say that in many ways it has dominated my life. I should certainly not be working in London otherwise.'

'You prefer the country?'

'Yes.'

'I've a cottage at Wilmington, in Sussex,' he volunteered.

'Near Eastbourne,' Anita said immediately. 'A beautiful spot.'

The inter-com went and Mrs Baxter's voice, raised in alarm, said, 'Mrs Richmond is here—she's not well and, oh! she's fainting.'

Ross Wyndham jumped to his feet.

'A friend of Glynis' as well as a patient. Three months' pregnant,' he volunteered, as he and Anita hurried into Mrs Baxter's office.

Jill Richmond was slumped in her chair, ashen-faced.

'Oh, Ross!' she cried, 'the baby.' Her gaze went appealingly to Anita. 'Please help me—' She made a helpless sign to convey that she was bleeding.

Without a word Ross Wyndham picked her up as though she were a child, and carried her through to the examining room, laying her on the couch.

'How long—when did this start?' he asked anxiously.

'Just a little, yesterday,' she replied. 'It seemed to stop—'

'Why didn't you send for me?'

'I—I didn't want to bother you . . .' She added piteously, 'Don't let me lose the baby.'

Anita knew there was no question of Ross Wyndham making an examination, or disturbing the patient in any way. Miscarriages, or abortions, according to the time factor, had to be left severely alone, until such time as the patient could have proper and sustained attention.

'It came on again just now . . . increasing. I was just going to pop in to see about—' she winced with pain—'about Glynis.'

'We're getting you into hospital straight away. I'll call an ambulance—'

'No; no! Alan won't be home until late, and there's Andrew—'

'I'll see to Alan and get in touch with Nanny . . . lie quietly.' He patted her hand and hurried into his consulting room, getting through to St Mark's immediately.

Jill looked appealingly at Anita. 'I'm so glad you're here . . . Ross is wonderful, isn't he?' She writhed, breathless.

Anita agreed. She had, from the start, been impressed by his gentleness, his calm which communicated itself to his patients, almost with a mesmeric quality. They openly adored him. Yet he could be firm, but never intolerant; and while he did not suffer moaners gladly, neither did he condemn them for their weakness.

He returned, his fingers going to the patient's pulse.

'We'll soon have you comfortable,' he promised. 'I've spoken to Sister Young, too. You will remember her; she looked after you when Andrew was born two years ago—my godson,' he added proudly. His voice was low and soothing.

'Thank you,' came a faint and resigned whisper. 'Could you—' she looked up at Anita pleadingly— 'could you come in the ambulance with me?'

Anita glanced at Ross Wyndham for his approval which he gave with a swift gesture and murmur of assent.

'And I shall be in to see you later on,' he promised Jill, 'when I've visited the two patients I operated on this morning.' He also suggested that Anita remained at the hospital until then.

Anita felt the thrill of an unexpected familiarity. In the past half-hour Ross Wyndham and she had become closer than in the previous month, and it was a closeness that held a subtle intimacy as though he had opened a door into his life which would never again be closed to her. A few minutes later as she got into the ambulance, she blessed this fragile girl who had contributed to the transformation.

By the time Ross Wyndham re-joined them in the silence of the hospital room, Jill had lost the baby and was under sedation.

'Sister told me,' he said, looking across to the armchair by the bed where Anita kept vigil. He sighed and shook his head. 'I'm so sorry.' A gentle protective expression touched his lips as he stood contemplating the sleeping figure. 'No reason why there shouldn't be more children,' he added softly. 'But we shall have to keep her under constant surveillance.'

The Staff Nurse came into the room, glancing

from face to face, saying swiftly, 'Good evening, Mr Wyndham.' There was unmistakable pleasure in the greeting. Ross Wyndham was one of the most popular consultants in his field. She added, 'Nurse Fielding and I were at the Westbrook together.' She was studying Jill as she spoke, solicitude tinging professionalism.

'Hospitals are full of coincidences,' Ross Wyndham said. 'You're satisfied with your patient?'

'Yes; it was complete . . . no complications.' Which meant that the foetus and membranes had come away whole.

'So I understand.'

'Would you like anything? Coffee?' she offered. She was an attractive, clear-eyed girl of twenty-four, quietly efficient and well-liked. She and Anita had been on the same wave-length and were good friends.

'Thanks, no,' Ross Wyndham said. 'We'll eat first. Mr Richmond will be in later on. I want Mrs Richmond kept in for a few days—at least,' he added.

Anita was hearing the echo of those words, *'We'll eat first'*. There was the implication that the word 'together' might be added.

Once outside in the long corridor, with its pale off-white walls, air of remoteness and noiseless activity, Ross Wyndham said, 'There's a pleasant restaurant near here; I suggest we go there. You must be hungry.'

'I hadn't thought of food until now.'

'Neither had I . . . once the patient is satisfactory, things change.'

Anita indicated her uniform. 'I hardly think being dressed like this is quite the thing for a restaurant.'

He looked as though it couldn't have mattered less, but said, sensitive to her point of view, 'I know what . . . we'll go back to Harley Street. Mrs Smithers will have a meal ready and I insist on your joining me. I don't want the reputation not only of overworking my staff, but of starving them, too!'

'But—'

'No argument,' he said with a wave of his hand as he whisked her off to his Daimler before she could protest further.

A little shiver of excitement made Anita's flesh tingle. This was the last thing she had foreseen, and it astonished her. Was he merely being polite and considerate? Grateful because she had been helpful to Jill Richmond who was a personal friend? Impossible to tell from his expression, which was pleasant and relaxed as though he were, in fact, following his inclinations with the ease of one accustomed to being obeyed, or having his own way.

Harley Street was silent and deserted—a world apart, full of tragedy, apprehension, and in curious juxtaposition, relief and happiness. As Anita stepped into the familiar long hall, a coolness struck and a fanciful mood made her think of the glory that had once surrounded the house, as though voices echoed from the past when one family, with possibly liveried servants, had lived there. What famous people had walked through that heavy front door? climbed the impressive stair-case? Now all was hushed; the patients had vanished like ghosts, leaving a stillness almost painful. The waiting-room door was closed. She looked up at the lofty ceiling, at the beaded cream panelling which bore testimony to a former elegance.

As though reading her thoughts, Ross Wyndham said, as he ushered her into the lift, 'When the place is empty, I always wonder what story it has to tell.'

'I was just thinking along those lines.'

When they reached his flat Anita felt unashamedly nervous. This was a new world to her, and Ross Wyndham an imposing figure in it. A little of the awe crept back. He was her employer and she did not underestimate his position. She looked around her, at the near-circular hall, its walls hung with signed prints of landscapes and hunting scenes. A large antique gilt-framed mirror created a feeling of even greater space as it reflected the light, and the carefully arranged flowers which stood on a Sheraton table set in an alcove.

Mrs Smithers, a small, wiry little woman with bird-like face and perceptive eyes, appeared noiselessly. Ross Wyndham made the introductions, his manner easy, friendly as he added, 'Will you look after Nurse Fielding? . . . dinner in half-an-hour?' It was not a command, rather a request.

Anita was taken to a cloak-room that seemed larger than her own sitting-room.

'You will find everything you need,' Mrs Smithers said politely, inwardly asking herself why her employer had brought his *nurse* to dinner unexpectedly. He never entertained the staff; not the right thing at all, she thought disapprovingly.

'Thank you.'

Anita realised that she had not even taken her

handbag with her to the hospital, and while she hardly required make-up, now, she would have liked some lipstick. As it was, she splashed a little water over her face and left it at that. She was trembling slightly; her thoughts chaotic, unprepared for the tumult within her. Being with a man when there was work to do was one thing; being his guest was another. What would they talk about? Would she bore him?

Mrs Smithers was hovering discreetly nearby when she left the cloak-room, and said quietly, 'If you'll come this way.'

'This is a beautiful house,' Anita said pleasantly, feeling that she was in the presence of a schoolmistress.

'Once owned by Mr Wyndham's grandfather,' came the proud reply. She led the way to the drawing-room where Ross Wyndham got to his feet as Anita entered.

'Now, what will you drink?' He made a gesture towards the table where decanters glistened, the cut-glass sending off prisms of light in a blaze of colour. 'Sherry, dry Martini . . . I'm good at making those, I warn you.'

'I think I'll stick to sherry, please,' Anita answered cautiously.

'Dry?'

She nodded.

He poured it out and a whisky for himself, then sat down facing her, looking into her eyes as they took the first sip.

'I—I haven't even my handbag with me,' she said, a trifle nervously.

'You mean you left it in the rooms?'

'I'm afraid so.'

'That's simple; we can get it when I run you home
. . . or do you want it now?'

'I just wanted my lipstick,' she confessed.

He studied her unnervingly.

'You don't need it, I assure you. And I'm in no
way averse to make-up unless it is plastered on, but
your lips are—' he hesitated slightly—'red.'

'They don't feel it!' A little of the tension drained
from her as she looked around. It was a large room,
with floor-to-ceiling windows, its height consider-
able. And while it had the comfortable atmosphere
of a bachelor apartment, nevertheless it was artistic, with shades of dove-grey and lilac predomi-
nating. Cushions in bright colours adorned the
sofa, and deep armchairs offered relaxation.

'I appreciated your going to the hospital with Jill;
you gave her just the support she needed,' he said.

His voice was warm and made Anita glow. There
was something about him as he sat there, glass in
hand, completely at ease, that sent a strange un-
familiar sensation over her body which might have
become an object that he was drawing to him like a
magnet. Was this thrilling awareness infatuation?
She knew only that being with him, alone, represented sudden ecstasy, robbing her of the ability
even to speak, fierce emotion bringing near-panic.

'Are you all right?' The question was asked with
anxiety.

Anita struggled back to some semblance of normality, managing to smile and insist that she was
perfectly all right, just admiring her surroundings.

'You know, Nurse—' He stopped and made a
wry face. 'I can't keep calling you that. Let it be

Ross and Anita outside practice hours. I get very tired of formality; I'm a rebel from it in fact.' He held her gaze intently. 'It will give our relationship a new dimension. I feel I *know* Anita.'

Ross. Anita liked the name and was flattered by his suggestion.

'I agree about formality. It freezes me,' she admitted.

'Heaven forbid . . . What do you want from life?'

She tried to escape from the effect of his deep, resonant voice as she said, 'Something very commonplace, old-fashioned and, I suppose, considered dull!' Colour crept into her cheeks. 'I want, eventually, to be married and have a family. I suppose I feel cheated because of all that happened in my childhood. I've no desire to be a strident female carrying a banner.'

'Which is altogether refreshing,' he said.

'But I want to be good at the job. Not a suet-pudding wife, forever humped over the kitchen sink—' she stopped—'and I mustn't get on my hobby-horse.'

Ross smiled. 'You have my approval. I see too much misery not to appreciate a woman who has her priorities right.' He was weighing up every word she uttered, conveying the impression that it was of importance to him. Again she asked herself if he was merely being charming and polite.

'And you?' she said, a trifle challengingly, thinking that he had achieved the height of professional ambitions, having his FRCS and MS, with a professorship also to his credit.

His answer was to haunt her in the near future, but at that moment it gave an edge to the conversation, 'I rather think that fate dictates the pattern,' he said somberly. 'May I ask if you are likely to be married in the near future?' He appeared to hang on her reply.

'As things are at the moment,' she said honestly, 'no.' Even as she spoke she thought of the past, and her first love, Kenneth Lawson—Dr Lawson. Was it, she often asked herself, the magic which left the memory lingering like a fantasy? Yet the emotion now surging upon her was, by comparison, a tornado against a summer breeze.

'There *was* someone, but we lost touch and—'

The door-bell rang like a fire alarm in that moment, preventing further explanation.

Ross gave an explosive, '*Damn!* I'm not expecting anyone, so it must be an emergency—'

But it was his step-mother, Janet, and Glynis Morgan, the latter coming in like a tidal wave, crying, 'Ross! I couldn't wait to—' She stopped, her expression of happiness and excitement changing to obvious disappointment, even annoyance. 'Oh!' she murmured rather sullenly, giving Anita a critical stare. 'Not another emergency! I thought specialists were immune—'

Ross cut in with the necessary introductions, without filling in the background of Jill Richmond's case. Anita assumed that he would choose the right moment to impart the news of her miscarriage, since Glynis would obviously be upset to hear of it.

'How do you do, Nurse Fielding?' Janet Wyndham said, her voice warm and friendly. 'I always think that nurses should have medals as large as gongs!' Her blue eyes twinkled, her smile was broad. She was a woman of sixty, with a melodious voice, pink-and-white, finely-textured skin and dark, grey-flecked hair.

'You weren't expected home until the weekend,' Ross said to Glynis who had slipped her arm through his, the gesture possessive.

'Since we were flying back from Singapore, we got an earlier flight. I thought I'd surprise you, and I'd had enough. I've missed you.' She looked up at him adoringly.

Anita's heart sank. Guardian and ward? At that moment it appeared to be something far deeper as she watched the glances they exchanged. Any hope that the visit might be brief was shattered by Ross insisting that they remained for dinner. Glynis accepted with alacrity, Janet equally eager.

'I thought we might go to Monk's Corner this weekend,' Glynis suggested, her voice wheedling. 'Oh, Ross, it's so good to be back!'

Ross had rung for Mrs Smithers and was telling her of the dinner arrangements, which she accepted without demur, accustomed to erratic catering.

Anita lapsed into silence. She had nothing to contribute to a conversation which continued to revolve around Glynis—her trip, her desires, her intentions. Finally, however, Glynis paused and then exclaimed, 'Well, Nurse Fielding, how do you like working for Mr Wyndham?'

Anita met a pair of bright, calculating grey eyes, set in a face that was undeniably beautiful, with high cheek bones and well-marked brows. Glynis had an air of confidence quite disconcerting; was obviously intelligent, impetuous, and determined. Anita found herself thinking that she could be a formidable enemy, and a shiver of dismay touched her because she was aware of a veiled hostility which would be difficult to combat when working in the same practice.

'I'm very much enjoying it,' she replied.

'Ah well, I shall be back on Monday.' The words held a note of challenge, bringing with them a strange foreboding.

Ross said unexpectedly, and to Anita's amazement, 'Since it seems we are going to Monk's Corner this weekend, why don't you join us?' He looked at Anita as he spoke, almost as though willing her to accept.

'Oh, yes, do,' Janet exclaimed approvingly. She liked Anita instinctively, thinking that her expression was full of character and compassion. And Ross would not have even invited Anita to dinner unless regarding her with respect and friendliness.

Anita hesitated.. Since Glynis had made her feel an outsider even in the space of a few minutes, how would she, herself, face up to such an attitude during an entire weekend? But defiance surged in a wave of resolute determination and, smiling, she said, 'I'd love to do so.'

'Splendid.' Ross spoke with hearty approval.

Glynis didn't utter a sound for a second or two, and then adroitly turned the conversation back to herself, suggesting that they have a party over the weekend, and go to the Congress Theatre in Eastbourne, or the Theatre Royal in Brighton.

'Why not pop up here to the Barbican while you're at it,' Ross commented dryly. 'I can't possibly get down until late on Friday, and I'm operating early on Monday morning.'

'*Work!*' Glynis made a grimace. 'It ought to be abolished by law!'

There was a sudden tense silence.

Ross's voice was a trifle curt as he said, 'You don't *have* to do any, Glynis. It was your choice to—'

She cut in swiftly, her expression contrite, 'You know how I'd hate not to be in the practice. It's just that the weekends at Wilmington are never long enough.'

'Ah!' Ross said.

Anita thought that Janet looked on with faint apprehension, glancing from face to face as though trying to guage the mood of each, and smiling faintly at Anita almost with apologetic indulgence for Glynis's extravagant utterances and attitudes.

Glynis talked all through dinner which was a delicious meal of fresh salmon followed by strawberries and cream. And when later, after coffee, Anita announced that she must be leaving, Ross said immediately that he would run her to her flat.

'Is it far?' Glynis asked pointedly.

'Just off Baker Street—Hill Mews,' Anita added.

'It doesn't matter how near, or how far, it is,' Ross spoke with quiet authority.

Anita knew that for her to protest, or talk of walking (as she did every morning and evening) would be futile.

'Then I suppose you had better drop us off on your way,' Glynis said with faint resentment. 'I am tired, and don't fancy even the short walk . . . I can't believe I'm back . . . Really *home*.' She got to her feet and moved to Ross's side, conveying an intimacy of which Anita was acutely aware.

'I hate dragging you out like this,' Anita said to Ross some short while later, when Janet and Gylnis had been deposited at their flat. 'After all, it is such a short distance and—'

'It is a pleasure,' he assured her without the words appearing facile. 'Besides, I want to see where you live, or you will have the advantage over me!'

When they reached the quaint cobble-stoned mews, with its old-world atmosphere and bright window-boxes, Anita said in a breath, 'Would you like to have a look at my flat?'

'Very much.'

Her key went into a sapphire-blue front door at the side of a pink-washed, bow-windowed house. A short flight of stairs brought them to their destination.

'This is charming,' Ross exclaimed as they crossed the threshold.

It had a studio air; with book-lined walls, a few carefully chosen pieces of reproduction furniture, and bowls of daffodils to bring it to life. White and pale jade formed the colour scheme in the sitting-room, a bow-fronted, leaded window emphasising the picturesque setting.

'Can I offer you a brandy?' Anita inclined her head towards the drinks tray.

'Just a small one,' he agreed.

Having taken the drink, he stood looking around him approvingly.

'This has character,' he said warmly. 'Quite unique, and while it is small, one doesn't feel cramped.' He sat down with her, seeming thoroughly at ease. 'I'm so glad you're coming to

Monk's Corner,' he said. 'You'll like it.'

'I'm sure I shall.'

'Perhaps we shall have an opportunity really to talk,' he suggested tentatively.

Anita smiled, her expression doubtful.

'Does one ever manage to discuss philosophies and ideas?' she asked, 'or find the person with whom one is in sufficient harmony to make it possible?'

'Meaning that we are always compromising?'

'Something like that.'

He held her gaze with a certain admiring intimacy which quickened her heart beat, emphasising the fascination of his attractive personality and her own vulnerability.

'I don't like the implied concession,' he said, a trifle belligerently.

'We seldom, if ever, get all we hope for, Ross,' she said, the use of his name lighting a spark between them that flamed into desire.

The room was in semi-darkness, illuminated only by the lights of London that turned the sky to a pink glow; the traffic's roar a mere rumble, that became part of the silence rather than a discord.

'Thank you for this evening,' he said tensely. 'I'd better be going.'

As he got to his feet she switched on a desk lamp and stood beside him, their nearness awakening a surge of emotion. Her gaze was raised to his and their eyes met in half-questioning appeal.

'We'll have to discuss details for the weekend,' he said jerkily.

She saw him to the front door and to his car, standing there in the blue darkness, her lips parted temptingly, her eyes dark and passionate.

'Goodnight, Anita,' he whispered softly.

She watched him drive away, and it was as if her heart went with him. She did not know what tomorrow would hold, only that her life would never be the same again.

When she returned to the flat it was as though his ghost remained there; the echo of his voice like the strains of a great symphony, stirring her as emotion surged in a crescendo of longing that became an exquisite form of pain. What did he really feel, or think? Was his interest in her a form of curiosity that allowed rein for his charm? She had heard nothing to suggest that his relationships with women were suspect, as was the case with many of his colleagues. Equally, there was nothing that placed him in the category of the confirmed bachelor. But, then, what did she really know about him? Mrs Baxter and Emily did not voice their opinions, so she had only the eulogies of the patients, who were naturally prejudiced by his skill, and care of them. Ross, the man, was an enigma and she told herself that she would do well not to allow imagination to run riot.

She doubted the wisdom of accepting the invitation to Wilmington, but emotion overruled caution and Glynis's attitude had seemed to throw down a silent challenge. Here, in the silence and seclusion of the flat, she was able to see it all in perspective and criticise her impetuosity. However, there was nothing she could do to reverse her decision. Fate must take its course. The question was how to combat her own weakness in the face of his powerful attraction and magnetic influence.

And as Anita got into bed a little later, Glynis was saying to Janet, 'I think it's very stupid of Ross to have invited Nurse Fielding to Wilmington. She isn't the type he ought to employ anyway.'

'Because she's young and attractive?' Janet smiled wryly.

'Nothing of the kind! She's a *type*. The *good* nurse; self-sacrifice written all over her. She'll dote on him, and drive him mad!'

Janet shook her head in disagreement.

'I'd certainly agree that she is a good nurse, but don't underestimate her! It's my guess that she's more than capable of standing up for herself. Nothing weak in *that* face. I liked her.'

'You like everybody.' It was a gruff sound.

'On the contrary; but I don't *dis*like anyone without just cause—a very different thing.'

'All the same, mixing business with pleasure never works—you've said so yourself.'

'That's true; but there are always exceptions.' Janet's voice hardened slightly. 'I hope you're not going to be difficult over Nurse Fielding. Ross won't tolerate friction.'

Glynis tossed her head, eyes flashing. 'What do you take me for? Give me credit for some common sense. I shall be sweetness itself to your dear nurse, believe me.'

Janet looked uneasy. She was beginning to discover a malicious streak in Glynis that distressed her. Suddenly the peaceful atmosphere which she had previously taken for granted vanished, and she was left with a feeling of anxiety and foreboding.

*   *   *

Friday turned out to be one of those stressful days, when Ross was called to do a Caesar on a colleague's patient and, in addition, Jill Richmond continued to bleed, thus needing a dilation and curettage for further investigation.

Ross said to Anita in the middle of the afternoon, 'I'd hoped to run you down to Wilmington, but—'

Anita said immediately, 'Far better for me to drive down; there's the return journey to consider, and I must get back on Sunday evening.' She paused, remembering that he had told Glynis he would be leaving then.

'That goes for all of us,' he said with a smile.

Would Janet and Glynis be travelling in his car? Anita asked herself, knowing that the last thing she wanted was to accompany them were this so. Already the aversion to Glynis was building up, much to her own annoyance.

'You have a five o'clock consultation—Mrs Barton.'

He made a somewhat desperate gesture. Mrs Barton didn't want the child she was expecting and, much to her chagrin, there were no valid reasons for a termination. She was petulant and uncooperative, demanding tablets for her morning sickness, which Ross steadfastly refused to prescribe.

'A luxury I could well do without . . . Do you swim?' he asked irrelevantly.

Anita laughed.

'Yes.'

'I've an indoor pool,' he explained. 'I find it about the most healthy exercise there is. One is either standing or sitting in this job!' He looked at her intently. 'By the way, Janet and Glynis will be arriving at Monk's Corner around five-thirty. No need for you to wait for Mrs Barton—you get away early. I've got to have a word with Stephen Morris after I've seen Mrs Barton. Thank heaven he's only in Wimpole Street. I shall be on my way immediately after seeing him—probably beat you to it, after all!'

'And I'll be on *my* way *after* you've seen Mrs Barton,' Anita said decisively.

'I think Glynis has invited one or two friends to join us,' he said. 'Yes, I know! The next patient . . . we don't want to run late today.' Again he held Anita's gaze and she turned swiftly as emotion swept back, engulfing her, wiping out time and place as she hurried away, pausing outside his consulting room door, confused, heart racing. Her awareness of him brought an excitement over which she had no control, leaving her helplessly involved, and filled with a yearning both physical and mental.

'In a trance, Nurse,' Mrs Baxter said crisply as she crossed the wide hall to her office.

Anita forced a laugh. 'Something like that . . . Probably a Friday afternoon feeling.'

'Particularly as you are going to Wilmington . . . Mrs Woodstock is waiting.'

It wasn't, Anita thought, what Mrs Baxter had actually *said* that mattered, but what she had left unsaid. Her faint smile masked disapproval.

Anita reached Wilmington just before seven that evening, feeling the tension drain away as she looked around her at its quaint village street, remembering the days when she used to stand on the top of Windover Hill, glimpsing the distant sparkle of the sea beyond the Cuckmere, and gaze at Alfriston nestling snugly in the river meads, the magnificent panorama of the Sussex Downs embracing Firle Beacon vanishing into infinity. Her heart seemed to miss a beat as the past rushed up at her and she thought of Kenneth Lawson. 'Lost touch,' she had said to Ross. Rather had it been an explosive recognition of temperamental disharmony, the memory of which hurt from time to time. Kenneth had been a senior registrar at the Mansfield Hospital where she had trained. His parents lived at Eastbourne. It had been first love; and she had had only a few innocuous flirtations since then until now, when Ross seemed to have taken possession of her life, blinding her to a world of reality and common sense.

She found Monk's Corner from the directions he had given her. A Georgian house, its flat white windows set in slate-grey stone, giving an air of charm and elegance. It was tucked away down a winding lane and stood back, hidden from the road. She took a deep breath as she turned into the drive and observed cars parked in the near distance. Ross *could* have arrived first, she told herself, unless Stephen Morris had kept him. And to her delight she saw his car near the garage, apprehension, nervousness vanishing. This was the beginning of adventure, why not go eagerly to meet it instead of conjuring up nameless fears?

The front door stood open, the sound of voices coming in a wave of sound as she entered the large hall—a room in itself—bright with flowers, brass and copper which decorated a Sussex grate, where logs burned to counteract any evening chill in the air, and give a welcome.

Ross saw her instantly and came to greet her. They looked at each other with a familiarity that made the house seem home.

'I hoped you wouldn't be late . . . good journey?'

'Wonderful, and knowing the way helps . . .'

Jakes, who ran Monk's Corner with his wife, took her case.

Ross said, 'You must tell me about your Sussex days, Anita. I'm curious.' He stopped, then, 'Ah, Kenneth . . . let me introduce you. Nurse Fielding, may I—'

Anita betrayed a mixture of fear and elation as she gasped, '*Kenneth!*'

'Anita . . . I don't believe it!'

Ross's voice cut into the sudden electric silence.

'I take it,' he said almost curtly, 'that you two know each other.'

And for the first time Anita heard a note of sarcasm, even anger, in his voice.

CHAPTER TWO

ANITA stared at Kenneth in amazement. He was the last person she had expected to see, and for some indefinable reason, faint apprehension touched her. She didn't want any complications, and Kenneth was not the type to be ignored. Equally, she was aware of Ross's somewhat hostile attitude towards their meeting. But she managed to say smoothly, 'Kenneth and I worked at the same hospital.'

'And we lost touch after you left,' Kenneth observed reflectively.

Ross flashed Anita a glance which reminded her of their conversation at the flat when she had confided that there *was* someone, but 'we lost touch'. It left her with a feeling that she was on trial.

Glynis sidled up to Ross at that moment, having assessed the situation.

'A reunion?' she exclaimed, adding teasingly to Kenneth, 'I've never heard you speak of Anita.' She managed to inject a note of mystery into the comment.

'And I've never heard Ross mention Anita, either,' Kenneth countered with a faint chuckle.

'That,' Anita flashed back, 'is because nurses are part of the furniture—particularly in Harley Street!' She deliberately forced a note of banter into her voice.

'Isn't that a contradiction in terms?' Kenneth retorted. 'You are *here*.' The implication was obvious.

Glynis scowled. She resented Anita's presence enough without having it stressed by Kenneth, who subtly highlighted the fact that Ross and Anita were on sufficiently friendly terms for her to be his guest.

Janet joined them, brightening visibly when told of Kenneth and Anita's friendship. She was very fond of Kenneth, and glad that Ross shared her regard for him, and his abilities, so that their friendship had grown, despite the fact that Kenneth lacked the ambition to launch out on his own, remaining a senior registrar on the firm of a consultant acquaintance of Ross. It struck her that it might be ideal if he and Anita re-discovered each other. She could not help being an incurable romantic while, nevertheless, having a common-sense view of situations. Her remarks were apt, light-hearted, ending on the practical suggestion that it was time for drinks.

Glynis said somewhat surprisingly, 'Renewing old acquaintances calls for champagne, Ross.'

Ross replied swiftly and with faint irritation, 'Jakes is *serving* champagne.'

That, Glynis thought, was obviously in Anita's honour. One look at Ross's expression warned her against comment. But her turn came when the champagne had been poured and she said with a deceptive smile, addressing Kenneth and Anita, 'May this be the first of many glasses you have together. It is always good to meet old friends again.' She gave a little giggle. 'Boy-friends, girl-friends—'

Ross gave a suppressed snort.

'My dear guardian can be very stuffy sometimes,' Glynis said.

Anita found her gaze drawn to Ross who seemed to have put the world between them. A short while later, they stood alone together, while Kenneth, Glynis and Janet wandered out on to the patio which partly encircled the house.

'Strange that I should know Kenneth,' Ross said tritely.

'Life *is* strange; nothing ever written about it is too fantastic. And the medical world, after all, can be a very small one.'

'This isn't the scene I had envisaged,' he said somewhat aggressively.

Anita looked up at him; his eyes met hers half-questioningly, half challengingly.

'But it is a very beautiful one,' she commented evasively, moving nearer to the open French window and looking out over a panoramic view of the countryside. 'Wilmington,' she added. 'And the Long Man of Wilmington, carved in chalk into the Downs—'

'I'm not interested in the history of the place,' he said hoarsely, 'but in *you*.'

There was a moment of breathless silence before she said involuntarily, '*Ross!*' Her voice was shaken.

'Were you in love with him?' The words came explosively.

Glynis's laugh shattered the mood as she and the others returned to the room. 'More champagne, Ross,' she exclaimed, 'and Anita's glass is empty.'

Kenneth moved to Anita's side, wanting to be alone with her.

'Why did you vanish?' he asked.

'Because one cannot live with indecision for ever,' she replied honestly.

'Meaning that you didn't want to marry me, *or* to sleep with me,' he suggested bluntly.

Her reply was as honest as possible. 'I wasn't sure about either, which seemed to prove the futility of our relationship. I thought absence might help.'

'And did it?'

'No; I drifted.'

'Meaning there's not been anyone else?' His voice was sombre.

'I just haven't met anyone.' She looked across the room to where Ross and Glynis were talking, unsettled by the fact that, even at that moment, she wanted to be in Ross's arms.

'Oh, *Anita*,' Kenneth said almost sadly. 'What a mess we made of things.' Then, as though regretting the statement, added, 'I ought to have put up a fight.'

'Yes,' she admitted simply.

A light came into his eyes and then dimmed.

'We shall have to see,' he said.

A matter of days ago her life had been devoid of any masculine influence, Anita thought. She had cherished the calm detachment which was now threatened by emotional turmoil, as she recognised the intensity of Ross's attraction, and the nostalgic memories revived by Kenneth's presence. The two men were totally dissimilar, but she could not deny Kenneth's rather elusive charm.

On the surface the evening, and during Saturday, appeared to be highly successful, but beneath the laughter there was tension which manifested itself in brief periods of silence, and a wariness that made Anita feel she was under surveillance as the two men focussed their attention upon her, to what, she realised, was Glynis's chagrin. Janet steered them through the difficult patches, her good humour breaking down barriers and curbing Glynis's tendency to make barbed remarks aimed in Anita's direction.

'Do you practise here at all?' Anita put the question to Ross at dinner on Saturday evening.

'Not if I can help it,' he replied with a wry smile. 'But we *do* sometimes get the odd emergency.'

'Because you are so popular in the district, and let friends take advantage of you,' Glynis flashed at him. 'I think they've got a cheek. Kenneth agrees with me.' She shot Kenneth a somewhat belligerent look. 'Don't you?'

'I think Ross needs a break when he gets down here,' Kenneth answered somewhat evasively.

'The medical profession never give a straight answer to a straight question,' came Glynis's swift retort.

The telephone rang, making Anita jump.

'I don't *believe* it!' Glynis exclaimed.

But it was an emergency. Ross had taken the call in his study, and returned to the dining room, grave, and shaking his head.

'You spoke too soon,' he said, looking at Glynis. 'That was Philip . . . Fay's had a fall. I must go at once. Paul, their doctor, is on holiday and the locum's out on a case.'

Janet gasped, 'Fay must be seven months pregnant by now.'

Anita said swiftly, 'I can be of use. It won't take me a minute to change.'

Ross nodded and Anita hurried upstairs.

'But—' Glynis cried, protesting, and then looked at Kenneth who sat silently and a little glum.

Ross collected his emergency bag and he and Anita drove off.

'Is it far?' Anita asked.

'A couple of miles . . . Apparently Fay fell down some steps in the garden.' Ross was thinking aloud. 'We may have to get her into hospital.' He gave Anita a sideways glance in the approaching twilight. 'I'm glad you're here.'

'So am I,' she agreed.

'Philip and Fay Adams, as well as their doctor, Paul Renwick, were the first friends I made after I bought Monk's Corner,' Ross explained.

Anita felt a stirring of emotion and swift desire which conflicted with the seriousness and urgency of their mission. The evening air was pure and intoxicating as it wafted in from the open windows, bringing the scent of wild flowers, and the tang of the sea. Late spring diffused a blue darkness over the landscape, while the temperature borrowed the warmth of summer. But her mood soon changed as they reached the Adams' house, Orchard Farm, a white-washed thatched cottage lying at the foot of the Downs.

Philip Adams' expression was one of near-panic as he greeted them, accepting Anita's presence blindly.

'Thank God you're here . . . she's in pain and

very shocked. Mrs Baker and I managed to get her to bed,' he explained as he hurried towards the staircase, Ross and Anita following.

Fay lay back against the pillows in a quaint raftered bedroom. She was twenty-two, flaxen-haired, with large blue eyes, and normally fostered the illusion of a Mabel Lucy Atwell character. Now she was white, tense and frightened, as she cried, 'The *baby*—' A spasm of pain contorted her features, and she gasped for breath.

Ross glanced at Philip. 'Leave us,' he said with gentle authority. 'I'll call you . . . this is my nurse,' he added, indicating Anita.

Philip nodded, desperate in his helplessness, as he went reluctantly from the room.

Ross made a thorough examination. Fay was in a state of shock, her temperature subnormal, blood pressure low, respiration shallow and rapid. She was also, to his dismay, having premature contractions. He and Anita exchanged significant glances, and while they both knew that babies had an amazing ability to survive even severe blows to the mother (being cushioned by the amniotic fluid), nevertheless shock was another matter.

Ross took Fay's hand reassuringly. 'Relax all you can; you're not injured in any way.'

Anita found pads, towels, and most of the necessary things, grateful that the bathroom was adjoining, and housed many vital items.

Fay cried, 'My *back* . . . pain.' The words came in a spasm of apprehension.

Anita went to her side, holding her soothingly and with sympathy.

Fay went into labour a little while later. There

was no question of being able to get her to hospital. She bore the ordeal in a state of confusion, seeming at times to be unaware of all that was happening, as she clung to Anita who cleansed and attended her, slipping back into routine as though never having left hospital. And all the time she was aware of Ross's skill as he manipulated the delivery until, to their horror, the child, a boy, was stillborn—two months' premature.

'Oh, *no*,' Anita whispered, as she and Ross looked at the tiny mite which almost maintained its position as though in the womb.

Ross's face was ashen. A shuddering sigh escaped him as he shook his head in despair.

To their relief Fay remained seemingly oblivious of her surroundings, giving only a whimper as the placenta came away, her body exhausted, her mind still confused.

'I'll give her an injection of ergotamine,' Ross said in a low voice to Anita. 'Contract the uterus, and then I'll sedate her.'

Anita nodded, attending to her duties, stunned by the tragedy of it all.

'We've got to get a nurse from somewhere,' Ross said jerkily, moving from the bed having given Fay the injection.

'I could stay tonight,' Anita volunteered.

'*No*,' he said sharply. 'I've contacts in Eastbourne if we fail locally.' He dragged his gaze away from the now shawl-wrapped little shape placed nearby, and out of Fay's vision should she suddenly become aware of her surroundings. But her eyes were blank as, a short while later, she took the tablet Anita gave her and sipped the water mechanically. Then, mercifully sedated, she slipped into sleep.

It was two o'clock in the morning when Ross and Anita finally left Orchard Farm. Nurse Helston, who lived locally and was known to the housekeeper, Mrs Baker, came to the rescue, and was already installed. Philip stood at the front door, seeming to have aged ten years, his eyes hollow and full of shadows.

'Fay *will* be all right?' he asked Ross for about the tenth time. 'I mean, when she *knows*—another shock—' his voice trailed away desolately.

'Your support and understanding will be her best tonic,' Ross assured him. 'I'll come in later, and get in touch with the locum. There's nothing to worry about physically,' he stressed.

'God knows what I should have done without you,' Philip said. His fair hair was ruffled by the breeze; he had the bronzed complexion of a man who loved an outdoor life, and who farmed because his roots were in the land, as had been his father's and grandfather's.

Ross and Anita drove back almost in silence until they were in sight of Monk's Corner, then Ross said, 'One never feels that enough has been done; and that there ought to have been *something*—'

Anita was immediately defensive. 'It was a straight-forward delivery . . . she wasn't even torn—'

'I should think not,' he flashed, 'at twenty-eight weeks.'

'I've seen gynaecologists who shouldn't be delivering the carry-cot, let alone the baby!' Her voice was fierce and without humour. She wanted to add that his technique had been extremely skilful, but avoided stating the obvious. 'They are a happy couple?' The question came irrelevantly.

'Ideally happy; suited in every way.'

Anita nodded, and then gave a little shiver. 'Mrs Richmond's miscarriage, and now a stillbirth . . . I seem to be a jinx.'

'Nonsense!' he shot at her. 'And you're wasting your talents with me. You must know that? It was an abrupt, unexpected remark.

'That is up to me,' she said. 'I wanted a break from actual nursing.'

'A sad way for us to spend part of the weekend.' He sighed as he spoke.

'But had the baby lived, a wonderful way,' she commented. The intimacy of their task during the past hours seemed suddenly a bond, drawing them closer, and when a matter of minutes later, his key went into the lock of the front door, he turned and looked down at her in a long intent gaze that sent a thrill over her body. She thought that he was going to lower his lips to hers, but as he was about to move, the door opened and Glynis said, 'We began to wonder if you had got lost.' And while her tone was light, the gleam in her eyes was piercing and critical, as she glanced at Anita—a glance which Ross failed to see. She rushed on as they went into the drawing room, 'I thought you might like coffee. And I got Jakes to leave some sandwiches. How *is* Fay?' She dropped her voice on a note of concern.

Ross told her.

She looked shocked. 'How *dreadful*.' She raised her gaze to his, her expression gentle with compassion. 'I'm so sorry . . . I know what these cases mean to you; besides, Philip and Fay are our *friends*.' She gave every word significance and Anita felt that they were chosen to impress Ross, rather than part of any deep sympathy.

He nodded, then, 'Coffee would be very welcome,' he said quietly.

'You know I worry about you,' she said softly.

He put a hand on her shoulder. 'I know,' he said.

Anita felt suddenly an outsider. It was a sharp painful awareness of not belonging.

'Thank you all the same,' she said when Glynis was about to pour the coffee for her. 'If you don't mind I'll go straight to bed.'

'Are you sure?' Glynis was expansive because she wanted Anita out of the way.

'Thank you again,' Ross said, 'for all you've done.'

Anita just gave a little uncertain smile, said goodnight, and went to her room. It was a moment of intense loneliness that conflicted sharply with the events of the evening. The silence both inside the house, and in the deep stillness of the countryside, seemed like another presence that made even the beating of her heart noisy. After what seemed a very long time she heard muffled footsteps and whispered voices from the landing. She lay wondering just what the relationship was between Ross and Glynis, and if their marriage was a foregone conclusion. The thought of Kenneth obtruded for a second, as she asked herself just what her feelings were for him, and how meeting him again would affect her future? Not being able to answer either question, she fell asleep.

*   *   *

Sunday brought the lazy drowsiness, the sound of church bells, the sense of peace which was part of the countryside.

Ross was standing in the sunlit hall as Anita went downstairs to breakfast, his gaze holding hers as she walked towards him. Her heart quickened at the sight of him. He looked impressive and very much the master of the house—relaxed, wholly in command, and considerate, too, as he asked, 'Did you get any sleep?'

'Early tea awakened me, or, rather, Mrs Jake's knock . . . any news?'

'I've spoken to Philip. Fay took it bravely. Time and rest are the two essential things now.'

Anita gave a sigh of relief.

They went into the Sheraton-furnished dining-room which looked out over a walled-in garden, now bright with spring flowers and surrounded by budding and blossoming trees. Janet, Glynis and Kenneth were already at the table, breakfast being a movable feast. Ross led the way to the sideboard which offered a variety of dishes. Anita's hunger was more emotional than physical, and she took a small portion of scrambled eggs. Ross helped himself to bacon, sausages and tomatoes.

'I always have a proper breakfast on a Sunday,' he said with satisfaction.

'And,' Glynis chimed in, 'on any other days when you can put your wretched patients on ice!' Then, as Anita sat down at the table, she asked, 'How are you feeling after your errand of mercy?'

'Obviously not very hungry,' Kenneth observed, looking at Anita's plate.

Ross might not have heard that as he said to

Glynis, 'I don't deal with "wretched" patients except in the unhappy sense! Perhaps it is your holiday in the sun that has made you seem resentful of them. Or is it my imagination?'

Glynis flushed. 'No,' she admitted. 'But I don't seem to have had any time really to talk to you.'

Janet gave a short chuckle. 'You can put a full-stop after the word, "time". You've hardly been back—'

Glynis cut in, 'We didn't count on last evening's crisis!'

'Neither did Fay,' Ross said quietly.

'But she's all right,' Glynis countered. 'You *said* so when I asked you this morning. I mean, just before breakfast.' She was like a persistent child not wanting to have any further anxiety.

Kenneth spoke up, 'In a case like this it is a matter of degree.'

'Exactly,' Ross agreed.

'Will you be going to Fay this morning?' Janet asked.

'Yes; about eleven-thirty. I've had a word with Paul's locum.' Ross paused. 'I'd like you to come with me, Anita.' He made it sound like a request, adding, 'I know Fay would want to thank you.'

Anita gave her assent, making it plain that she would very much like to visit the patient.

'*I'd* like to see Fay,' Glynis exclaimed. 'Can I come, too? I was very concerned about her last night.'

'I appreciate that,' Ross said. 'But Fay will not be seeing anyone for a day or two. Sometimes, what people *don't* say can be as painful as saying the wrong thing. Next time we come down it will be a different matter.'

Glynis sighed, then suggested, 'I'll take Kenneth into Eastbourne—go for a walk on Beachy Head . . . Or would you rather read a book, Kenneth?' she added, laughing as she spoke. She looked at Anita, 'Had Kenneth always got his nose in a book when you knew him before?'

There was a sudden silence.

Anita replied, aware of Ross's intent gaze upon her, 'Yes, as a matter of fact, he was a reading addict—if there is such a thing! So you still are?' she added, smiling in his direction.

'People's habits change very little,' Kenneth commented. 'Or, for that matter, people themselves. They only delude themselves that they do.'

Anita lowered her gaze; the words held a significance which she felt Ross was swift to appreciate.

Glynis stared at Kenneth. 'And how much do you remember about *Anita*?' Her voice was challenging, her awareness of Ross's interest uppermost.

'You wouldn't expect me to answer that question,' he answered subtly.

'More coffee anyone?' Janet asked, conscious of the sudden tension and a little baffled by the look of resistance on Ross's face.

'On second thoughts,' Glynis announced pertly, 'I shall sun-bathe; it's hot, and since we mostly have our summer in the spring, I'll take advantage of it . . .' She flashed Kenneth a friendly, half-teasing look. 'You can join me if you like—*and* read a book; or have a swim.'

'We'll be back well in time for drinks,' Ross said. 'You're right, Glynis—it *is* hot.'

'Back for drinks,' she echoed, moving nearer to him as he got up from his chair. 'You didn't say morning or evening! Or even which year!' She put a hand on his arm. 'Don't be late,' she added softly, 'will you?'

He gazed down at her indulgently and a knife seemed to turn in Anita's heart. But the depression was short-lived and, as she and Ross set out for Orchard Farm a little later, Anita felt a wave of happiness that was in tune with the beauty of the late April day. The fresh young green of the trees, the cottage gardens, the sensuousness of the warm breeze, made her say, 'This *is* a perfect morning, Ross.'

'You make my name seem—' He broke off self-consciously.

'Seem—what?'

'Significant, almost musical. I like it.'

Faint colour crept into her cheeks; her awareness of him intense. He glanced at her. 'You look like Spring,' he added surprisingly. 'That crisp white blouse—and little blue jacket—' He broke off almost as though regretting the note of intimacy, his expression suddenly inscrutable. 'I'm afraid you haven't had much chance to spend any time with your friend—renew the old acquaintance,' he said.

'One evening will hardly make much difference.'

'Meaning there is plenty of time ahead.' His voice was faintly sardonic.

Emotion gave a note of defiance to her voice.

'Exactly.' Why, she asked, the sudden change of mood? Certainly nothing she had said, or done, could be responsible. The brightness of the morning dimmed, her nerves becoming taut, apprehension taking the place of a former confidence.

Fay seemed to have a porcelain frailty about her as Anita greeted her some short while later. Her smile was wan and the tone of her voice unnatural, as she endeavoured to avoid self-pity.

'You were so kind, so helpful,' she said, holding Anita's hand.

'And you were so good,' Anita insisted.

'It all seems like a nightmare,' she said.

Anita made no attempt to offer any sympathy, only understanding. She just met Fay's sad gaze and nodded.

'It's terrifying, the difference twenty-four hours can make,' she went on. 'Philip's been marvellous . . . How long are you staying at Monk's Corner?'

'Only until this evening.'

'Please come to see me again when next you're here.'

Anita told herself that there wouldn't be a 'next time'. Ross's attitude was incomprehensible and she could not stand conflict. But she said, feeling an instinctive bond with Fay, 'I will.' They might have known each other for years.

'Nurse Helston is very capable.' Fay spoke in a flat monotone. 'Ross is wonderful, isn't he?'

Anita recalled Jill Richmond making precisely the same remark. Now she wanted to challenge it!

'A very fine gynaecologist,' she replied evasively.

'I was so lucky that he was here.' There was a

second's pause before she echoed painfully, '*Lucky*.' Her eyes filled with tears; her voice rose. 'Why, oh *why*, did it have to happen?' she asked. 'Everything was so wonderful—'

'It will be again,' Anita said gently.

A trusting expression came into Fay's blue eyes. 'Tomorrow . . .' She squared her shoulders. 'Philip mustn't see me . . .'

'Fay is better than I dared hope,' Ross said, on the homeward journey. 'She liked you very much, and was so appreciative.' His manner reverted to normal, leaving Anita baffled and longing to read his thoughts.

'I admire her courage, especially when she's so low physically,' Anita said, feeling that the golden brightness of the day mocked the sadness at Orchard Farm. 'Back to London this evening,' she added reflectively.

'Yes.' He uttered the word on a sigh. 'The weekends are all too short.' His features were set in determined lines. Every now and then he shot her a sideways glance, as though trying to make some assessment.

At last the car stopped at Monk's Corner in a clearing near the garage, which was screened by trees. There, he slid from the driving-seat and moved swiftly to open the door for her. She got out and stood beside him, inadvertently brushing her arm against his, the impact like an electric shock, so that instinctively she raised her gaze to his, aware of the passion that suddenly darkened his eyes. For a second he hesitated, then leaned forward, parting her lips in a fierce possessive kiss, his arms tightening suffocatingly around her body, desire sharp and demanding. After a moment and almost abruptly he released her.

She swayed, shaken and bewildered, her heart thumping.

CHAPTER THREE

KENNETH appeared as Ross and Anita were moving away from the car. He was wearing a bath robe and said, 'I'm going to the pool! Glynis is still lapping up the sun.' His gaze went to Anita. 'How about joining me?'

Anita was still trembling from the ecstasy of Ross's kiss, but she managed to say brightly, 'I'd like to.' She glanced up at Ross.

Kenneth added swiftly, 'The three of us could—'

Ross cut in, 'I've a telephone call to make. I'll come along later.' With that he hurried ahead of them into the house.

'I'll go and change,' Anita said. 'Where *is* the pool?'

'Oh, of course, this is your first visit here!' Kenneth studied her as they sauntered to the front door. 'I'll wait for you,' he said as they reached the hall. 'Janet has gone to visit a friend, by the way.'

Anita nodded. 'Won't be more than a few minutes.'

'I remember how quickly you used to change, no matter what the occasion,' he commented, looking at her with admiration. 'A great asset in a woman.'

She smiled and hurried up the stairs, returning promptly, an attractive robe covering her swimsuit.

The pool was built as an annex, with a domed glass roof and panelled glass sides which slid back like double glazing to give the illusion that one was out of doors. The pool itself was a Mediterranean blue, flanked with a wide tiled terrace, on which attractive white wicker chairs and tables were arranged, together with a few brightly-covered lilos, creating an attractive leisure centre.

'Luxury,' Anita said with appreciation.

'Ross never does anything by half,' Kenneth replied.

Anita felt a little tremor, the memory of Ross's kiss still burning her lips. She threw off her robe and stood in her cream-and-scarlet swim-suit, which revealed every line of her slim perfect body.

'You've grown even lovelier, Anita,' Kenneth said quietly.

'And you still say the most extravagant things.'

'Are you glad to see me again?'

'Yes,' she admitted honestly, and dived into the clear sparkling water, racing the length of the pool, and then floating luxuriously by the time he reached her side.

'Still elusive,' Kenneth exclaimed.

'Cautious, perhaps.' Her laughter echoed through the silence.

'When do you go back?' He was suddenly serious as he floated beside her.

'Tonight.'

'We must meet again.' There was a note of urgency in his voice.

'I never make appointments in swimming pools,' she teased.

'You'll make one this time,' he insisted.

They reached the shallow end and stood side by side.

'When, Anita?' He was persistent.

She looked at him, feeling the warmth of a friendship renewed, together with the nostalgic memories of first love.

'Not this coming week,' she murmured, slightly breathless.

'Then tomorrow week?' he insisted, 'we may not have any time alone together before we leave.'

'Very well. Tomorrow week.'

'I could pick you up at your flat. Six-thirty.'

She agreed.

'And seal the bargain,' he murmured, and before she could escape him, put his arms around her and his lips on hers.

Ross's voice cut through the silence, 'A very pretty little scene.'

He stood at the edge of the pool, having come in through an open window. His eyes seemed to pierce hers as their gaze met. But it was impossible to gauge his reactions, for his expression was inscrutable, his manner disarming.

'And a very delightful pool *for* such a scene,' she said, heart racing, a bold challenging mood possessing her. 'I'll race you both—two lengths.'

Ross flung down his robe, standing rather like a bronzed god in his dark trunks; his smooth lean body that of an athlete, without a spare inch of flesh.

Anita cut expertly through the water, straining every sinew to win, succeeding at the first length, but beaten at the second; as finally she stood, her hand on the edge of the pool, breathing heavily. Ross had won, for he was a strong swimmer who always gained the advantage, even from Kenneth.

'That was foolish,' Kenneth admonished her.

'Why?' Ross's voice had an edge to it.

'If Anita hasn't done any swimming recently . . . It isn't everyone who has an indoor pool, after all.' His voice held a mixture of concern and envy.

Anita was aware of the sudden tension between the two men and felt a flash of power normally foreign to her.

'I'll get my reward,' she exclaimed.

'How?' Ross demanded, the word like a shot from a pistol.

'By floating to the deep end and lying there in peace for a few minutes. The water's so soothing—and a perfect temperature.'

'I've ordered the drinks out here,' Ross said, 'so I'll give you exactly *two* minutes.'

Their gaze met through the mirror of mutual annoyance, yet each conscious of the other's body and the overwhelming emotion neither could conceal.

Kenneth swam a few strokes away. He was content to have succeeded in getting Anita to have dinner with him and was busy planning ahead. His pulse was racing at the memory of their kiss, and he was a little amazed by his own determination. In addition, he asked himself where Ross fitted into the picture, allowing for Ross's relationship with Glynis.

'On second thoughts,' Anita said, 'I think I've had enough exercise.' She lowered her gaze and turned away from Ross. It was impossible to escape his dark penetrating eyes, which were smoulderingly accusing. She swung lithely up to the tiled terrace and swiftly donned her robe.

'Anita—' Ross spoke her name sharply.

And at that moment Glynis called out from the entrance, 'Why didn't someone tell me you were *here*?'

'Kenneth said you were still sunbathing,' Ross answered.

'I fell asleep,' she explained somewhat petulantly. 'You've obviously finished your swim.' She looked towards Kenneth. 'I didn't know you were going for a swim.' She spoke in an aggrieved tone.

'I told you,' Kenneth said pleasantly, 'but you were too absorbed with your sun-tan.'

'How long have you been back?' Glynis's gaze went to Ross.

Ross murmured something inaudible, his attention directed towards Jakes who was carrying the drinks tray, which he put down on one of the tables.

'Ah, that jug of Pimms looks just what we need!' he exclaimed. 'Thank you.'

'I don't like Pimms,' Glynis pouted.

'Then there's plenty else to choose from,' Ross replied. He appeared not to notice her mood, but Anita realised that, in a matter of minutes, Glynis had completely changed the atmosphere, rather like a spoilt child. There was suspicion in her manner and a beady critical expression on her face as she turned in Anita's direction.

'Can I give you a Pimms No 1?' Ross addressed Anita, his voice distant and ultra polite.

'Please.' Anita felt shaken, the memory of Kenneth's kiss was like a sword flashing between them.

Glynis refused a drink, and sat sullen and silent, infuriated because Ross ignored her.

'We're very late for lunch,' she grumbled finally, as Janet came into view and joined them.

'I refuse to be rushed on a Sunday,' Ross said. 'Mrs Jakes knows that, and understands. If you're hungry, have an olive, or some of the—'

Glynis cut in, unable to curb her emotions as she gave way to a fierce jealousy. 'I hate olives!'

Ross's expression was severe. 'Your sunbathing and sleep haven't done your temper much good,' he said sharply, finding an outlet for his own mood.

Janet upset her glass at this juncture, and then misjudged the distance between it and the table, so that it splintered on the tiles.

'At this rate I shall need spectacles,' she laughed.

'Nonsense,' Glynis countered. 'You just don't *look*.'

'Probably not.' Janet drew her hand across one eye as if to remove a cobweb.

Anita watched vigilantly, remembering the incident later on.

The rest of the day did little to restore the harmony. There were awkward silences and time dragged. Only Glynis seemed satisfied as she continued to sunbathe, telling herself that probably Anita would be too bored to risk a second visit.

From time to time Ross's gaze met Anita's, and emotion, part desire, part uncertainty, created an uneasy atmosphere that set her nerves jangling. She was almost relieved when, after tea, she was able to say, 'I think I'll leave about six, if that is all right. One can never gauge the traffic, but . . .'

'Pity you came by car,' Glynis said, 'or Kenneth could have taken you back.'

Janet laughed. 'We've almost a fleet of cars!'

Kenneth had maintained a discreet silence, but broke it by saying, 'We could, of course, all meet up and have a meal *en route*.'

Again Glynis spoke up, 'Why don't you and Anita do that?'

Anita hastened, 'I would like to get back early.' She gave no specific reason.

'So would I,' Ross announced.

No more was said and Anita saw Ross alone for only a matter of seconds before she left.

'Thank you for the weekend,' she said formally.

'It has not been as I planned.' His voice was edgy.

'Fay Adams's tragedy could not fail to cast its shadow,' Anita said tactfully.

'I wasn't really thinking of that at the moment . . . but, at least, you have met up with Kenneth again, so, from your point of view, coming here has been worth while.' The words were uttered slowly and deliberately.

Anita flushed and said with a trace of defiance, 'There's no question of his "making it worth while", but I'm glad to see him again.'

'That is obvious . . . I hope you have a good run back.'

'Thank you again,' she murmured.

Kenneth decided to leave almost at the same moment that Anita finally drove away.

'I've a shrewd idea they will stop *en route*,' Glynis said knowingly to Ross. 'They make a good couple. It's time Kenneth was married.'

Ross stared at her, his expression darkening.

'*Married!*' He made the possibility sound foreign.

'Why not? After all, they may have been lovers

for all we know. Catching up with each other again may be—'

'Conjecture is a waste of time.' He paused, his eyes critical and hard, 'You've been in a very unpleasant mood today. Why?'

Glynis knew Ross too well to try to pretend, or make excuses. 'The weekend seemed terribly boring. I'm afraid I didn't make the necessary effort.'

He looked down at her. 'I don't like to see you behaving badly, and there was no reason why you should have been bored.'

'I'm sorry, Ross.' It was a low regretful sound. She slipped her arm through his. 'It's lovely to be on our own. Let's go for a walk?' Her smile was beguiling. 'You don't *have* to leave so early.'

He gave a little indulgent nod. 'Very well . . .'

Glynis congratulated herself on getting out of a situation that could have been explosive, while recognising that she'd played her hand very badly. She also realised that it would be extremely foolish to repeat the performance.

Monday morning offered Anita a challenge. It marked the return of Glynis to the practice and, quite probably, the end of her own supremacy. And while Glynis could not pull rank so far as her particular job was concerned, she could do so through the importance of her relationship with Ross.

Ross greeted Anita as he entered his consulting room, with his customary courteous if absent-minded 'Good-morning'. If anything, she thought, he seemed a little more distant, so she plunged straight into the problems of the day.

'Mrs Sheriden's doctor telephoned—Dr Brown—for an appointment.'

'*Fleur.*' He was instantly alert.

'Dr Brown said that it was urgent. Mrs Baxter managed to make the appointment for eleven.'

Ross looked upset and anxious. Obviously Fleur Sheriden was a friend as well as a patient, Anita thought.

'Dr Brown doesn't panic,' Ross was saying, thinking aloud rather than talking. 'He's a fine general practitioner, and will come with her.' Ross had not yet sat down in his chair, but did so, putting his elbows on his desk, clasping his hands and staring straight ahead. 'Eleven,' he murmured. 'We've got a heavy list today.'

'Is Mrs Sheriden young?' Anita felt a strange sensation churning in her stomach.

'Thirty. Just divorced her husband. No children. I've known her for years.'

He made it sound as though he met her when she was in her cradle, but Anita was used to the fact that men, in general, had no idea of time.

But Fleur Sheriden arrived alone. Dr Brown had been called to a coronary. Anita thought that she was one of the loveliest women she had ever seen, with a pale nut-brown skin, dark silken hair, parted in the middle, and falling to her waist.

'I haven't seen you before, Nurse,' she said to Anita, and while she smiled, there was a shadow in her large dark eyes, and distraction in her manner.

Anita reflected, as she showed the patient into Ross's consulting room, that he was surrounded by attractive women, and a strange pang hurt her as she contemplated Fleur Sheriden. Ross's attitude was full of concern as he held her hand for a fraction of a second longer than necessary.

Fleur Sheriden burst out, 'I've had a lump in my breast—watched it grow—for over a year.'

'*What?*'

Anita moved out of sight, while able to hear what was being said.

'I know; I've been stupid. Dr Brown was very angry . . . don't you be, Ross, *please*. I've always told myself that if I thought I had cancer, I'd keep it to myself because the cure is so often worse—'

'It's not for you to make judgments,' Ross cut in. 'Lumps in breasts don't have to *be* cancer and, even if they are, they can be removed and allow people to live a full life span. Good heavens, Fleur, you're an intelligent woman—' He paused, then, 'Let me have a look at you . . . Nurse?'

Anita moved forward and opened the door of the examining room, where Fleur Sheriden undressed for examination. The lump in her breast was visible.

'I know,' came the almost apologetic remark to Anita, 'I've been silly.'

'We all are, in one way or another,' Anita said with understanding.

Ross made his usual thorough examination, straightened himself, and said, 'I think we can deal with this right away. A cyst which I'll aspirate.'

'What does that mean?' Fleur Sheriden asked.

'Draw off the fluid.'

'Oh!' The lift in the voice was noticeable.

'The fluid will have to be analysed, of course,' Ross hastened.

'And I won't need an operation?'

'One step at a time,' he said.

Anita prepared the hypodermic with which he infiltrated the area, anaesthetising it, and then, a matter of seconds later, penetrated the cyst and drew off a straw-coloured liquid which was put into a small phial.

Fleur sighed as he pulled the sheet up to her shoulders.

'Oh, Ross,' she whispered, 'What would I do without you?'

'Probably behave like a responsible woman,' he replied. '"Watched it grow for a year", indeed!' He made a gesture with his hands to convey amazement and disapproval. 'What is the good of our *telling* you women to examine your breasts, and make sure you haven't any lumps! Wasting our breath,' he added in exasperation. 'Now get dressed . . . Thank you, Nurse.'

'Such comforting people, nurses,' Fleur Sheriden said, with an appreciative smile in Anita's direction. 'And, heaven knows what people like you would do without them!' She grinned at Ross as she spoke.

'For once today, I agree with you,' he said unexpectedly, as he left them.

'Is this all, if it's only a cyst, Nurse?' Fleur Sheriden looked at Anita anxiously once they were alone.

'You'll have to ask Mr Wyndham the questions,' Anita answered with a smile, while knowing that it would be a question of follow-ups should the fluid prove negative. She re-set the trolley; sterilised the instruments, made up the examining-couch with clean linen, and when summoned to Ross's room found that Fleur Sheriden was still there.

'I wanted to say goodbye, and thank you,' she said. 'And I know I've been here far too long.' She looked at Ross with obvious gratitude and intensity. 'And we'll have dinner on Wednesday,' she murmured, moving to the door.

Glynis appeared as the door opened.

'I've only just realised you were here,' she said. 'I was having a coffee and—' She looked from face to face, half-suspiciously.

'And now I'm going,' Fleur Sheriden said, smiling. 'Did you have a pleasant holiday?'

'Splendid; but it's good to be back . . . Your next patient has been waiting at least twenty minutes,' she said to Ross.

Fleur Sheriden laughed. 'Patients take the day off when they visit specialists—particularly in Harley Street.'

'Libel,' Ross countered. 'Show the next patient up,' he said to Glynis and, without shaking hands with Fleur Sheriden, gave her a rather lingering look of understanding, said goodbye, and turned back into his consulting room. There he sat down at his desk and said, shaking his head, 'I didn't expect this today.'

'It must be dreadful when friends are involved,' Anita commented.

He looked thoughtful, lowered his gaze, and then said heavily, 'Yes; yes, it is.' He went on swiftly, 'What are you doing this evening?'

'Catching up on all the chores I neglected over the weekend,' she replied a trifle breathlessly.

'I see.' His attitude suggested that the remark

was a dismissal of any invitation he might have made.

Anita thought swiftly and apprehensively of the following week, when she was to have dinner with Kenneth. And while she argued that her appointments had nothing whatever to do with Ross, nevertheless a tension surrounded the possibility of his knowing. And when the actual evening arrived, she found herself hurrying to finish her work, and to avoid any discussion with him about the hours ahead.

'Janet and Glynis are going to the theatre tonight,' he said casually, when the last letter had been signed and Mrs Baxter had collected them. 'Do you like the theatre?'

'Very much,' she said, 'provided it's a good play; but when it is not, I wish I had a knob conveniently to turn it off! At least one can do that with television . . . You won't forget that you have a nine-thirty appointment—Mrs Welby—in the morning . . . Oh! I haven't had time to mention Mrs Sheriden. I'm so thankful her test was negative.' Anita relaxed a little as she spoke, feeling that Fleur Sheriden would absorb his attention sufficiently for him not to discuss the present.

'Yes; that was a great relief. We'll have to keep an eye on her in future.'

Anita nodded, and moved to the door.

'Goodnight,' she said in a pleasant brisk voice, as she left him sitting at his desk, telling herself angrily that if she'd had any sense she would have mentioned Kenneth.

'In a hurry,' Glynis said, as Anita reached the main hall, ready to leave.

'Always in a hurry,' Anita retorted. 'Enjoy the theatre.' She knew the remark was indiscreet the moment she had uttered it, for Glynis said, 'Who told you I was going to the theatre?' She added before Anita could reply, 'Ross, of course.'

'Yes.' Anita was not in the mood to be provoked. 'Goodnight.' With that she opened the heavy front door and was away.

Glynis stood looking after her for a second, her thoughts racing. Suppose Anita was going out with Ross? For a while she argued with herself and then dismissed the possibility. But nevertheless, she said when she and Ross finally parted in the empty silence of the house, 'Anita was in a rush to get off tonight.'

'Really.' Ross's intonation told her nothing, as he hastened irrelevantly, 'I've an early appointment tomorrow—'

'I know . . .'

'Enjoy the theatre.' He smiled at her as he spoke.

'I don't like the idea of it without you . . . How about supper afterwards?'

'Not tonight . . . I've work to do and want a quiet evening.'

'Here?'

'Where else?'

'We haven't heard from Kenneth this week,' Glynis said. 'He usually rings.' She gave a little hollow laugh. 'Perhaps he's been in touch with Anita.'

Ross stiffened. 'You'll be late.' He ignored her remark about Anita.

'Did you enjoy your evening with Fleur?' The

question came abruptly. 'You haven't mentioned it.'

Impatience was creeping into his manner. 'There was nothing to mention. It was very pleasant.' He moved to the foot of the stairs and began to climb them, looking back at her as she reached the door. He was thinking about Kenneth and Anita, annoyed with himself because he could not ignore Glynis's remark.

'Ross?' Glynis's voice cut through the silence.

'Yes.'

'You seem faraway these days—why?'

'You imagine things,' he retorted gruffly. 'Don't keep Janet waiting.'

The door was half-open. She seemed about to speak, thought better of it, and left, telling herself that she would arrange an outing and get back on the old footing. A smile hovered about her lips. Nothing and no one would ever come between her and Ross.

Anita showered and changed to be ready at six-thirty. Her dress was striped navy-and-white with a touch of yellow, slim and elegant. Why, she asked herself, hadn't she wanted Ross to know that she was dining with Kenneth? One snatched kiss did not give Ross any rights or privileges, and she had no intention of being tied to anyone, in order that her movements would be monitored and provide a subject for conversation, and criticism.

Kenneth was punctual and greeted her with a certain air of familiarity, as though they had almost slipped back into the old routine.

'My word,' he exclaimed, 'you have a charming

place here. And you have the knack of always looking right for the occasion,' he added, moving towards her and implanting a kiss on her cheek—cautiously, and with discretion. 'I booked the table for seven-fifteen and the restaurant is just around the corner. Italian; small, but attractive.' He looked at her inquiringly, 'Do they know we're meeting?'

She shook her head. 'No. I didn't even say I was going out. Don't ask me why.'

'An aversion to comment or questioning. What we do is our business, after all.' He added, 'One gets very independent on one's own, and prickly when it comes to being cross-examined.'

'So I've found,' she agreed and their laughter mingled, easing the tension.

'Ross and Glynis were rather on edge over the weekend, I thought,' Kenneth observed. 'Even reunions need a period of adjustment, although their parting had merely been a matter of months. He's very protective towards her.'

'I'm not fond of poultices,' Anita exclaimed, jealousy prompting the remark.

'That's an old-fashioned word! So you don't want to be protected?'

'I'd rather be challenged,' she said.

'I seem to remember that, and failed at it.'

They sat and had an aperitif, talking of work, emotion, filling in the gaps of their respective experiences, and then walked quietly to the restaurant, with its red-and-white striped canopy, tubs of brightly-coloured flowers and welcoming entrance. *La Giaconda* was picked out in gold lettering above the doors, and there was a festive air as they went in, to be greeted by a beaming owner whom Kenneth knew. A cold buffet adorned a long narrow table offering rich and varied dishes. The bar was set in a deep frame, like a painting, bottles and glasses sparkling.

'This is most attractive,' Anita said appreciatively, taking in the royal-blue and white decor; the shining mahogany panelling, with subdued bracket-lights to reinforce the candle-lit tables. The thought of Ross surged, bringing a pang. She studied Kenneth as they sat together, re-discoverng each other, enjoying the moments and remembering the past which had slipped elusively away.

'I almost didn't go to Monk's Corner that weekend,' he told her. 'Now—' A faint shadow seemed to cross his face.

'You regret having done so.' The words came swiftly and with a degree of dismay.

'Good lord, no! The reverse.' He sighed. 'I suppose I'm apprehensive . . . there's still something elusive about you, Anita.'

She lowered her gaze.

'Let's enjoy this moment without regretting yesterday, or worrying about tomorrow. I don't want commitments, Kenneth. I want a period of freedom before I settle down.'

At that he brightened. 'Then we know where we are.'

'And you don't want to—to marry?' she asked.

He hesitated for a fraction of a second before saying reflectively, 'No; no, I don't want to marry.' He added, relief in his voice, 'Not now, at any rate. Freedom is valuable.'

Anita echoed the word, while the thought of

Ross made it almost seem a misnomer. Why should it matter about keeping this meeting with Kenneth a secret? Obviously, if they continued to see each other, she would tell Ross of her own volition. The explanation suffced.

And at that moment Ross was saying to Mrs Smithers, 'Leave me a few sandwiches, I don't feel like a meal this evening. I've to go out a little later.' He spoke quickly and avoided her steady gaze, then returned to his study, murmuring, 'Goodnight', in a muffled, almost inaudible, tone.

Ten minutes later he found himself walking down Harley Street in the direction of Hill Mews. He was restless and nervy, and had been toying with the idea of visiting Anita from the moment they parted that evening. Of course she might be out, but the possibility did not deter him and he quickened his pace until he reached the mews and her flat. It looked attractive in the evening light, and he rang the door-bell with a touch of defiance. She might not have eaten, in which case they could go out to dinner at one of the many restaurants in the area. He stood, pulse quickening, looking almost mesmerised at the bell, hearing it, but receiving no answer . . . She was obviously out. Certainly not shopping, he argued, at this hour. Anger built up out of a disappointment he would not acknowledge. He didn't want to think of reasons for his coming there, or of excuses for the emotion now gnawing at him.

And then, as he was about to walk away, he saw Kenneth's car parked on the opposite side of the mews.

CHAPTER FOUR

ANITA felt absurdly self-conscious as she arrived at Harley Street the following morning. There was the usual rushed day ahead, with Ross operating at St Mark's from eleven until one, while, in addition, fitting in his private patients at his rooms. By the time he was ready to see Mrs Welby at nine-thirty, he had already visited an emergency haemorrhage and transferred the case to hospital for investigation. He arrived at his consulting rooms, somewhat breathless, grateful that Mrs Welby was a 'follow-up' after a Caesarian Section, prior to her going to California for an extended holiday.

Anita said, 'You've a few minutes . . . Coffee?'

'Please.'

Anita fetched the coffee, irritated by her sustained feeling of guilt in not having mentioned Kenneth. This, however, was not the time to bring up personal matters, but she was acutely conscious of Ross's almost suspicious gaze. There was something in his manner that made her uneasy.

'Tell Glynis to bring the patient in,' he said brusquely.

Glenda Welby, thirty-five, was a chattering woman who now behaved as though no one else had ever had a Caesar. She was too rich, too spoilt, and too pleased with Glenda. She went off into a long dissertation about the merits of her husband, the new baby (a girl whom she flatly refused to breast-feed), the nanny, the new house, stopping only when Ross said, with a patience he was far from feeling, 'Relax, Mrs Welby; you can talk when I've finished examining you.'

But she managed to burst forth, 'The scar's wonderful, isn't it? And my breasts—no trouble, the tablets—' There was a merciful pause.

Ross was, as a matter of fact, pleased with his handiwork where the scar was concerned. He'd seen some cobbled-up abdomens in his time!

A little later Mrs Welby departed, still rattling on about the holiday itinerary, and almost what she intended having for lunch, even as she went out of the door.

'Thank God she's fine,' Ross exclaimed on a sigh.

Anita smiled. 'Some patients make one tired before they speak!'

'Huh! And not only *patients*! I'm not in a particularly tolerant mood. Mrs Smithers begins her fortnight's holiday today. I hate the disruption.'

Anita said involuntarily, 'If there's anything I can do?'

'Wendy will still be coming in daily, and Glynis will keep an eye on things.'

'Of course.' Anita's lips felt stiff.

Then he seemed to relent, 'How about a drink this evening . . . we'll need one.' There was a faint note of sarcasm in his tone as he added, 'That is if you haven't any other engagement.'

'I'd like a drink,' Anita said, and went to fetch the next patient.

It was after half-past six that evening when

Glynis rang on the inter-com. 'You've still got Mrs Tregrain waiting.'

'I know.' His voice was regretful. 'Anita is seeing Mrs Allen out and can bring Mrs Tregrain back immediately . . . You can go,' he added. 'I didn't realise you were still here. I'll be along later. You and Janet begin your meal if I'm held up.' He paused, then, 'Oh! I didn't know the Spencers were joining us; but they'll understand if I'm late, anyway. Give me a little time to unwind.' He clicked off the switch, leaned back in his chair and glanced at the notes on his desk. Mrs Tregrain was a dysmenorrhoea case, having painful periods. Unhappily married; with a lover whom Ross regarded as a philanderer. And while Ross was used to hearing about misery and matrimonial troubles, he preferred not to deal with them at the end of the day.

Anita showed the patient in, knowing that there would be tears, even sobbing, and pleas for help, not on account of her physical suffering, but her emotional traumas.

'I *had* to see you,' came the opening words, even before Anita left them. 'I can't go *on*.'

'Mrs Tregrain,' Ross said with sympathy and a degree of firmness, 'we've thoroughly investigated you—uterus, ovaries, fallopian tubes—'

'It isn't *that*,' came the low wail. 'It's Max—he's gone. It's all over.'

Ross listened as he had listened on many previous occasions, knowing that he had gone as far as he could in trying to solve the problem, and that now it was time for drastic measures as he suggested, 'I think a Marriage Guidance Counsellor would be of greater help to you than I, at this stage.

I've satisfied myself as to your physical condition—'

'But talking to you *always* helps me . . . I couldn't go *on*—'

'Then,' he said firmly, 'you must allow me to be frank. You have lost nothing by the departure of this man; he's undermined your health, drained you mentally, physically and emotionally, without giving you a moment's happiness—'

'But I love him . . . I *love* him.'

Ross sighed inwardly. How often had he heard those words uttered in varying degrees of euphoria, fantasy, desperation and abject misery?

When Mrs Tregrain finally left, Anita murmured sympathetically, 'That was a long session.'

'I sit here,' he said, shaking his head, 'doing my damnedest to draw on every known philosophy, but I'll *never* understand women! They confound every rule in the book and, by heaven, they try my patience! Let's go and have that drink. I need one!'

Anita wanted to know at least a little of what had transpired.

'What happened in the end? Mrs Tregrain looked better when she left you.'

'The husband wants her back. I made her see that she has nothing to lose by giving it a try; and that self-pity won't get her anywhere. Also, that she owed her *marriage* something.'

Anita could not fault that. 'And is the dysmenorrhoea psychosomatic?'

'I think it is quite possible. In fact anything is possible where a woman is concerned.' His voice had an edge to it.

'We don't seem popular today,' Anita said. 'Perhaps you should have gone into a different

branch of medicine. Gynaecology offers you no
escape from women, after all.' She couldn't resist
the observation, 'Normally you appear to be ex-
ceedingly friendly towards them, to the point
where they are all a little in love with you.'

He made an explosive sound of denial.

'Nurses,' she countered, 'see almost *all* the
game!'

'Nurses only *think* they do.' His attitude was still
belligerent.

They went up to his flat a few minutes later, and
Anita sank into the same easy chair as on that other
occasion, which seemed a very long while ago and
was, in reality, only about ten days. In that time
Ross seemed to have taken over her thoughts;
thrown her into emotional confusion, and
awakened desires impossible to suppress. Now he
appeared to be studying her almost critically, his
expression a little wary, his approach tentative,
as though he was wrestling with some unsolved
problem.

'Sherry or—'

'Sherry, please.'

He poured it out, choosing whisky for himself.
The house seemed vast, silent, and empty.

She looked up at him as he remained standing
and, meeting her gaze, he said, the words abrupt to
the point of harshness, 'I called to see you last
evening, but you were out.'

Emotion whipped up anger as she countered,
'Which isn't exactly a crime.' But her heart and
thoughts were racing. Why should he have visited
her?

'Did I say it was?' He paused, his gaze unnerving,

his manner suggesting that he was waiting for an explanation.

She lifted her head a little higher and said smoothly, 'I was with Kenneth.'

'Was that why you didn't answer the doorbell?'

'I meant that we were having dinner together. At La Giaconda,' she flashed, eyes blazing.

'I see.' He sat down. 'I noticed his car.'

'Is this a cross-examination? I didn't know there was a law against my going out with anyone.'

The atmosphere was tense and challenging. Why the annoyance? she asked herself. Or was he possessive about everyone—not just Glynis?

'Why didn't you mention Kenneth? Why the secrecy?'

She said honestly, 'I was going to tell you; and I don't know why I didn't mention it beforehand, except that, after all, it has nothing to do with you.'

He looked at her, his eyes dark with passion. 'You know that isn't true,' he said hoarsely. 'It has everything to do with me.'

Anita stared at him, overpowered by his masterful tone and attitude.

'Or are you in love with him?'

'No; and I don't want any commitments—he knows that. Also, I resent your interference.'

His manner changed, his expression softening, '*Do* you, Anita?' His deep voice made the words a caress; there was no escaping him, and she had no desire to do so. Before she could even comment, she was in his arms, hearing him say, 'My *darling*.'

They made love as though it was both natural and inevitable; a moment towards which they had been walking since the beginning of time, without strangeness or reserve, as their lips parted and passion swept them on to fulfilment. His possession of her was absolute, his body hard, yet gentle, against her own, as she drew him closer until it seemed they became one. He murmured her name, and she, his, in a frenzy of emotion while clinging to him, her arms still around his neck, her head cradled on his shoulder. Neither needed words in those moments. It was enough that they were together. There was a stillness around them as they lay there; the traffic silenced; Harley Street deserted. Evening light pierced an aperture between the heavy, gold damask curtains, throwing a spear of silver across the large, high-ceilinged bedroom. Anita felt drugged with happiness, every nerve in her body alive to his touch. *Ross Wyndham*, whom she had once thought would not even recognise her in the street! Was she really there with him in that large luxurious bed?

'I don't want this to end,' he murmured, his lips against her forehead.

Reality rushed back, without killing the rapture, or marring that which had been. And when they parted it was with a look that held the promise of tomorrow. This time it was *his* car in the mews, as he took her to her flat and reluctantly drove away.

A strange calm descended upon her as she went into the sittingroom; a calm that nevertheless still held the glow of ecstasy. Had she dreamed that hour? Created it out of fantasy and desire? No commitments, she had said, yet didn't intimacy give her a sense of belonging? Could she ever accept it as a brief, passionate interlude? The thought of Glynis obtruded sharply, insistently.

Just where did she really fit into the picture? Self-critically, Anita shut her mind against any problems. Why deceive herself? She had secretly wanted Ross to make love to her; everything about him awakened a longing she had never felt for any other man. His kiss at Monk's Corner had been the thrilling prelude.

When she went to bed that night, it was to re-live every second when she lay in his arms. The echo of his voice whispering, *'My darling'*, thrilling her like music throbbing into the silence of a moonlit night.

As Anita walked to Harley Street the following morning, the day seemed part of some magic pattern that had suddenly woven itself into her life. The pavements were dappled with sunlight, the houses seeming taller and more imposing. Not even the traffic, moving bumper to bumper; the heat, or the noise; could dampen her enthusiasm. In a matter of minutes she would be seeing Ross. But, to her consternation, Mrs Baxter, with owl-like anxiety, imparted the news that Mrs Wyndham was with him.

He called as Anita entered the examining room, and she joined them, finding Janet seated in the patients' chair. Janet gave a little laugh and said, 'No, I'm not making history by being pregnant, it's just that I haven't much sight in my left eye.'

'And,' Ross said with mock severity, 'she has waited months before mentioning it.'

'I didn't want any trouble and, anyway, it was only just misty to begin with.'

Anita exclaimed, 'A week last Sunday, by the

pool! You dropped the glass because you didn't judge the distance to the table!'

'That decided me,' Janet admitted. 'The other eye is all right.'

'I'm not an ophthalmic surgeon,' Ross put in, making an assessment, and putting Anita in the picture. 'Martin Jayson is the man to see. Fine specialist. I've asked Mrs Baxter to twist his secretary's arm for an urgent appointment.'

Anita nodded. 'I know the name. I've heard you recommend him before.'

'All this fuss,' Janet murmured.

'It's your *sight*,' Ross emphasised. 'You must have had some symptoms.'

'Nothing alarming, and no pain. Lights sometimes at the edge of that eye, and the feeling of having cobwebs or lace in it. A smarting sensation. I did intend saying something before Glynis went away, but things were pretty hectic here . . . now, well, it *has* deteriorated, so I've come to you for advice.'

Ross shook his head. Anita knew he was disturbed, and her own mood of euphoria vanished into near depression. She had great affection for Janet, and felt that it was mutual.

Mrs Baxter rang through on the inter-com. Mr Jayson would see Mrs Wyndham at three o'clock that afternoon.

Glynis rejoined them in that moment, aware of all the facts, and feeling guilty because she had ridiculed the possibility even of Janet needing spectacles.

'I ought to have *noticed* that sometimes you missed seeing things if you looked the wrong way!'

Janet laughed. 'I could do that with two good eyes,' she said.

Anita suggested tentatively, 'If you would like me to go with you—'

'Where am I going?'

'To Harley House—just the top of the road,' Ross explained.

Janet smiled at Anita. 'It is very thoughtful of you, but I don't need a keeper yet!'

'And if anyone goes with you, *I* shall,' Glynis announced almost autocratically.

'Call in here on your way back to the flat,' Ross insisted. 'If I'm tied up, you can always have a cup of tea—'

'Provided I don't prefer something stronger!'

'We keep that, too,' Ross assured her with a smile, 'for special occasions.' He glanced towards a corner cupboard which discreetly served as a cock-tail cabinet.

When Janet had gone, Glynis moved close to Ross, looking up at him with wistful eyes, putting her hand on his arm beseechingly. 'It isn't anything *serious*. Say it isn't? Oh, Ross, it would be so dreadful—' Her voice broke.

A terrible sensation of isolation washed over Anita as she stood there, aware of a relationship between Ross and Glynis in which she had no part, and of which she was increasingly uncertain.

'It could be a cataract,' Ross suggested.

Glynis brightened. 'That's nothing in these days.'

'Until you have it,' he observed. 'But so much progress has been made in that field—' He put an arm around Glynis's shoulder, then pulled himself up sharply. 'Mrs Brent is waiting. Bring her in,' he added gently.

Glynis reluctantly left them and in the few seconds they were alone, Ross said, 'Glynis is devoted to Janet—' His brows were puckered, his voice low.

'We all are,' Anita murmured, but even in that moment of drama, she craved some sign from him; a look, a gesture; even a hint of remembrance. But he might have gone off into some foreign world where she could not reach him. A pang brought a sick sensation to her stomach, until suddenly, unexpectedly, he murmured, his gaze holding hers, 'I wanted to *talk*, but there's no time, and I'm lecturing this evening as you know.'

Anita rocketed from hell to heaven, ridiculing herself for the fact. The fierce desire almost alarmed her. There was something about him as he stood there, in his dark suit and almost dazzlingly white shirt, that enhanced his attraction, his dominance part of authority.

'Yes, I know,' she said.

He stretched out his hand and took hers in an almost painful grasp, as simultaneously Glynis opened the door. Even in a brief glance, Glynis was aware of Anita's slight confusion and the fact that she moved jerkily and abruptly from Ross's side. For an instant Glynis looked at her mockingly, then, having announced the patient, went swiftly from the room.

Anita found that mockery brought a reaction of fear, where jealousy might almost have been flattering. She saw Glynis alone a little later, and before Janet returned from her appointment.

'If we could compare the day book for tomorrow,' Anita said, forcing a smile.

'By all means.'

Glynis had an attractive small room a short distance from Mrs Baxter's. There she made endless cups of coffee and had, in fact, a domain exclusively hers. Her receptionist duties involved her in friendly contact with all the patients, many of whom knew of her connection with Ross, and considered her a great asset to the practice as a whole. Anita did not quarrel with this. She merely accepted the fact that Glynis resented her presence from the moment they first met, and suddenly had an uncanny intuitive feeling that she was looking at someone who was concealing a secret, and gaining power from the fact. A burning sensation flooded her body as she thought of the previous evening, and just what Glynis's reactions would be to the truth.

Glynis said unexpectedly, 'Do what you can to help Ross get away as early as possible tomorrow.'

'Tomorrow?'

'He's taking me to the Barbican.' Her smile was slow and self-satisfied. 'We've so many things to catch up on; plans to make,' she added significantly.

Anita felt empty and hollow; her heart seemed to be pumping in a vacuum. She would not be seeing Ross this evening, and now, with tomorrow booked . . . She managed to say, 'I'll do my best, but it is rather like asking me to change the tides.'

'Ah, well, at least you know how things stand,' Glynis said ambiguously.

Anita returned to Ross who had been writing a personal letter.

'Mrs Brent hasn't arrived.' Her voice was cool and factual.

Ross might not have heard her for, without a word, he drew her into his arms, his lips seeking hers in a long passionate kiss. In that moment all thought vanished at his touch, as she responded to his every movement, and need, until at last she broke away, her voice breathless, almost shocked, as she said, 'You've *patients*—'

'I can't see them when they are late,' he insisted, but, nevertheless, straightened his tie, squared his shoulders, and endeavoured to regain some semblance of control as he added, 'and if you *will* bewitch me . . . I've always regarded myself as a sane, sober man, well in command of my life! Now, I'm behaving—'

The inter-com went.

'Damn!' His voice was raised and impatient. 'Yes, Glynis . . . Oh. she has. Very well. Bring her in.' He turned back hurriedly to Anita, 'Darling, we could have dinner together tomorrow evening.'

'You're taking Glynis to the Barbican.'

There was a sudden awkward silence during which Anita felt that he wished to avoid comment or explanation, as he said, '*Tomorrow?*'

'So she said.'

Anita maintained a purely professional attitude and managed to be completely detached until well into the afternoon, when she burst out, 'Oh, *dear*! I wish Janet would come back.'

The tension eased and they were drawn back together by a mutual anxiety as Ross said,

'Martin Jayson is probably running late . . .

What a difference it makes on which side of the desk one is sitting!'

Anita softened, 'Yes, everyone is important to that someone who is waiting for news. And there's a story in every patient, quite apart from his, or her, medical history.'

Ross lowered his gaze for a second before adding, 'And in every doctor and surgeon, too.'

'To say nothing of nursing staff!' Anita forced an almost flippant note.

A frown hardened his lips, and narrowed his eyes. 'We are all interdependent,' he said shortly, 'and to ignore that fact is folly.'

'Except that some people make their own rules and live by them.' Pain, jealousy, found expression in the observation.

For a second they faced each other—at war.

'Surely that is *your* philosophy,' he countered cynically, 'since you don't want any commitments.' He stopped abruptly, adding, 'Yet I seem to remember your telling me the first night you came to the flat, that your ultimate objective in life was marriage.' His eyes looked deeply into hers, 'A conflict of views, and a direct contradiction.'

Colour dyed her cheeks. How could she say that it was only with Kenneth she wished to avoid commitments? Nevertheless she murmured, 'I was dealing specifically, not generally.'

He continued to hold her gaze, his own deepening as though he were looking into her heart, drawing her to him with inescapable passion, once again lost to time, or place.

'I shall remember that,' he whispered tensely, his voice seeming to hold a note of warning.

Janet returned just before Ross was due to go to a consultation in Wimpole Street.

'A cataract,' she said simply, as Anita and Glynis greeted her and they joined Ross. 'Mr Jayson was charming—wonderful. So understanding. He wants me to have the operation in June. My right eye is good, and I shall probably have a contact lens afterwards.' She added, 'It was a—a shock to begin with, and he allowed for that, too.'

'He will write to me,' Ross said, looking at her with affection.

'Cataracts are nothing these days,' Janet said brightly. 'One is always hearing about them; but I'm a bit young. I forgot to tell him that I injured that eye some years ago, or, rather gave it a blow . . . funny how, when you get in the patients' chair, you never remember anything you want to *say*, or even *ask*!' She gave a little laugh. 'When I think back, I realise that I ignored quite a few signs, and symptoms, during this past year or so . . . I'll only be in hospital a few days.'

'And,' Ross said warningly, 'will not be able to lift anything heavy, or to bend over, for a few weeks afterwards. No housework or cooking.'

'I don't do much of either.'

'You do when Mrs Woodstock isn't there to help you.'

Glynis looked immediately apprehensive.

'You mean—' she addressed Ross, 'you mean Janet will need *nursing*?'

'Good lord, no,' Ross replied. 'Just looking after, in the sense that she will need to have her bed made, bath drawn. No picking things up from the floor, or leaning over a sink for any purpose whatsoever—little things—'

Janet looked utterly disconsolate for the first time. 'In fact I shall be a thorough nuisance,' she said unhappily. 'That's what I mean by *fuss*.' A sick sensation churned in her stomach.

'Of course you will not be anything of the kind,' Anita assured her sympathetically.

Glynis was making rapid calculations and said in a resolute voice, 'I've got the perfect solution! *Anita* could go with you to Monk's Corner! She's the *ideal* person. We'll manage here, won't we Ross? And we can always call on Nurse Pettifer who, after all, has come to the rescue before.'

CHAPTER FIVE

ANITA felt that her heart had stopped beating as she heard Glynis's suggestion. It had nothing to do with not wishing to care for Janet, but everything to do with the expression in Glynis's eyes, and the feeling that she had an ulterior motive.

'Mrs Jakes would—' Janet spoke swiftly, a feeling of unease stealing over her.

'Nonsense!' said Glynis. 'You will need *companionship*.' She added flatteringly, 'Besides, Anita will give you confidence and *we* shall have peace of mind, too. Don't you agree, Ross?'

Ross spoke quietly, 'Yes. It's an excellent idea—'

Anita, fearful lest Janet might misconstrue her silence, hastened, 'If things can be arranged here, I'd love to go with Janet to Monk's Corner.'

Glynis smiled, and said on a little note of triumph, and as though Anita were not there, 'I knew Anita would be only too delighted.' She put a hand on Janet's shoulder. 'Now you need have no more worries or qualms about anything. That's settled.'

'You would be alone at the flat,' Janet suggested.

Glynis laughed.

'I shall be *here* practically all the time. And we can pop down at the weekends.'

The use of the word 'we', had never had more significance from Anita's point of view. She wondered what Ross was thinking, feeling? Glynis had taken over without any protest from him. Yet, in fairness, she told herself, what opposition could he have put forward, since Janet's welfare was involved? And who was Nurse Pettifer? Obviously someone who had worked for him previously.

'I must be off,' Ross said, 'or I'll be late for my consultation. I shall go straight on to the College of Surgeons.' He looked at Anita as he spoke.

Janet got to her feet. Something about Anita's expression troubled her, and she could not have said why. She looked from face to face. 'Thank you for being so helpful. And reassuring.'

'We'll have a real talk later,' Ross promised her.

'You'll be coming in after the lecture,' Glynis said naturally, and as though it were a foregone conclusion.

Janet looked at him; she had a 'please do' expression on her face.

Ross picked up his fountain-pen from his desk in a little nervous gesture. 'Yes,' he said jerkily. 'But it may be late.' He turned to Anita. 'Telephone Mrs Chard before you leave, and make an appointment. I want to see her.' Mrs Chard was pregnant and her blood pressure was too high.

'Not tomorrow,' Glynis butted in. 'You hate not being on time for a concert, so don't get cross!' Her smile was endearing.

Anita said crisply, looking at Ross, 'Then it will have to be Friday.'

'I leave it to you,' he said, and left with Janet and Glynis, whose arm slipped naturally through his.

Anita stood watching, beset by presentiment. Ross had made his lecture an excuse for not seeing *her* tonight, yet was able to call at Janet's flat—a fact Glynis had taken for granted. She squirmed at what she considered to be her own pettiness, but could not escape from the bleak fact. Mechanically she consulted Mrs Baxter, before making the appointment with Mrs Chard; tidied up Ross's desk, prepared the trolley for the morning, and put on the sterilizer, so that all the instruments would be ready for use. The rooms were empty and silent, and the ringing of the private line made her jump.

Kenneth said, 'Is the Big White Chief available?'

Anita explained.

'I wanted a word with him about a cousin of mine. And I *mean* a cousin!' Kenneth's throaty chuckle was infectious. 'What are you doing this evening?'

Anita prevaricated, and then, almost with defiance, admitted that she was not going out, nor seeing anyone.

'Then should I be welcome?'

Why not? she asked herself, refusing to become the woman sitting alone waiting either for the telephone, or doorbell, to ring.

'Yes; very welcome,' she said.

'It won't be until after eightish.' He added swiftly, 'I shall have eaten.'

'Then we'll have coffee and brandy! I've some left over from Christmas,' she added with a laugh, while feeling her spirits lift.

'Splendid! Tell Ross I rang.'

'Any message?'

'No; only that I'll contact him tomorrow.'

Glynis came into the room as Anita was replacing the receiver, glancing at the instrument with faint suspicion, aware that it was Ross's private line.

Anita made no comment.

'Some X-rays,' Glynis said, holding out a large envelope.

'Ah! Thank you.'

'I'm leaving now—so is Mrs Baxter, and Emily . . . what are you doing?' It sounded like an interrogation.

'Seeing that everything is in order,' Anita replied coolly.

'The conscientious nurse . . . Good idea of mine about Janet, don't you think?' Glynis sat down in Ross's chair as she spoke, picking up various objects on his desk and putting them down again with maddening possessiveness. The diary, calendar, clock, paper-knife. 'I gave him all these,' she confided smugly. 'He's very particular about his desk.' She spoke as though Anita knew nothing about the man for whom she worked. 'Oh, well, I won't hinder you. Roll on Friday—' She paused significantly.

'Friday?' Anita seemed to be holding her breath.

'We're going to Monk's Corner.' She got up out of Ross's chair as she spoke. 'I think it is at its most heavenly in early May—a fortnight can make a lot of difference at this time of year.' She smiled—a sly smile. 'But you'll be able to enjoy it in June, after all . . . Goodnight.' With that she went from the room.

And while she had not said a word to which anyone could take exception, Anita felt that an abrasive had been rubbed over her heart.

*   *   *

Kenneth arrived at eight-thirty.

'Been dashing about like a mad dog,' he exclaimed. Then, as he reached the sitting room, added, 'And I've been looking forward to this—' His laughter echoed cheerfully. 'And I don't mean the brandy,' he added, as Anita handed him the glass.

Her laughter mingled with his, as they made themselves comfortable in their respective chairs.

'Are you going to Monk's Corner this weekend?' she asked suddenly, cherishing the fugitive hope that he was, and that Ross and Glynis would not just be there with Janet.

He shook his head. 'On duty . . . why?' He looked at her speculatively.

'No particular reason. Glynis happened to mention that they were going.'

'Ross is able to have the best of both worlds,' he said thoughtfully. 'If I'd worked just that bit harder, and had more real ambition—'

Anita interrupted, 'Good heavens, it isn't too late for you to begin in private practice.'

He made a little deprecating gesture. 'I don't think I want the responsibility, to be honest. The obscurity of mediocrity—that's for me!' He looked at her long and earnestly. 'I'm glad I've found you again,' he said solemnly. 'I was a fool—*am* a fool!'

Anita said swiftly, not wishing to slide into any serious mood, 'Friendship is very valuable.'

'And *that* word is a misnomer if you like! So you don't want commitments; we neither of us do, as we were agreed; but that doesn't mean you don't attract me and—'

'Nothing Kenneth,' she hastened.

'The celibate life,' he suggested, his tone disbelieving. 'It would take a lot to convince me. You've changed; there's something about you. A glow, if you like. Any man would notice it,' he said, as though the revelation had just come upon him.

Anita laughed to hide the feelings that could well betray her.

'Now,' she exclaimed, 'we're back to what I told you when we were in the swimming-pool—that you still say the most extravagant things!'

'Only this time you know they are right,' he told her doggedly, and got up from his chair to cross to hers.

The door-bell echoed through the flat at that moment, before Kenneth could reach Anita's side. He stopped, an expression of disappointment and irritation crossing his face.

'Are you expecting anyone?'

'No,' Anita replied as she got to her feet, and before Kenneth could say any more, reached the front door and opened it.

Ross stood there.

Anita gave a little gasp of delight which almost immediately merged into confusion.

'I slipped away after the lecture,' Ross explained, stepping lithely over the threshold with an air of supreme satisfaction, adding swiftly, 'I thought we could have—'

Anita cut in hastily in case Kenneth might overhear, 'Kenneth and I are just having a brandy . . . do come and join us.'

A dark expression half-anger, half-accusation, spread over Ross's features as he said icily, 'Then I'm intruding—'

Frustration and disappointment whipped up the emotion that surged between them, making it impossible rationally to accept obstacles which threatened their desires.

At that moment Kenneth, recognising Ross's voice, appeared in the doorway of the sitting room, glass in hand. He looked surprised and faintly suspicious, but said with his customary ease, 'Ah! I wanted a word with you—rang you at your rooms earlier.'

'Really?' Ross walked down the short hallway and, in a few seconds, sat down in the chair Anita indicated, after accepting the drink she poured out. Then he asked smoothly, addressing Kenneth, 'What can I do for you?'

'Oh, I'll deal with it tomorrow when you've a moment . . . How did the lecture go?'

They were studying each other, not as friends in that moment, but as rivals; each unable to fathom the role of the other where Anita was concerned.

'Quite well.' Ross looked at Anita. 'I mustn't keep you if you are going out to dinner.'

'No question of that,' Anita hastened. 'We've both eaten.'

Kenneth said facetiously, 'I came for the brandy!'

Silence fell; the atmosphere tense. They plunged into desultory conversation of a trivial nature which dragged on awkwardly, until Kenneth said, 'I must be going.'

He emptied his glass and put it down on the occasional table beside him as he spoke.

Ross sat there—implacable.

'You're not coming to Monk's Corner this weekend, I understand,' he asked suddenly.

'No; working.' Kenneth turned to Anita. 'Are you going again?'

Ross answered immediately, 'Yes; Anita's joining us.'

Anita stifled an exclamation of surprise. It was the first she'd heard of it.

'No emergencies, I hope, this time,' Kenneth observed.

Anita was aware of a certain discomfort in Kenneth's manner, almost as though Ross's presence constituted a challenge he wished to avoid. It also struck her as being out of character. She offered another drink, inviting him to remain out of friendly politeness, but he insisted on leaving.

'I'll give you a ring tomorrow, Ross,' he said finally, getting to his feet.

'Do; we can talk then.' Ross's voice was pleasant and encouraging, relief at Kenneth's departure bringing a surge of goodwill.

Kenneth nodded and smiled weakly.

Anita saw him to the door and as they parted he said, 'I'm sorry not to be coming to Wilmington . . . just my luck to miss it when you are there.' He lowered his voice, 'And to have had this evening spoilt! But I knew Ross wouldn't go, so I might as well!' He kissed her hand. 'The car's further down the mews . . . Goodnight; I'll ring.'

Anita shut the door, beset by the strange feeling that she had been looking at a picture out of focus. For a second she stood taking a deep breath, the knowledge that Ross awaited her bringing a turbulent emotion tinged with apprehension.

'I'm afraid I drove him away,' Ross said, eyeing

her speculatively. Kenneth's leaving created an anti-climax. He had got to his feet and stood almost menacingly determined, as his gaze met hers and then lowered to her lips. 'I've very little time now,' he added, and paused.

'I didn't dream of your coming,' she said.

'Would you have invited Kenneth had you done so; or did he call unexpectedly?'

'I invited him,' she flashed back. 'You were booked, and will be tomorrow evening, also, so that—' Her voice trailed away; she wanted to challenge him that if he could go to the Barbican with Glynis, she was at liberty to see Kenneth; but she shrank from making the situation an issue.

Ross's near-anger died as though he'd no further desire to fight. He reached out and drew her into his arms, holding her with a stifling closeness as their lips met.

He wanted to stay, and as they drew apart the question was in his eyes, together with an accompanying reluctance to denigrate making love by according it only a few snatched minutes, when they both ached for the luxury of time.

'I ought not to have come at all,' he said roughly.

But even as he talked his arms enfolded her, their need for each other wiping out reality. He took her in the soft darkness of the bedroom, which was illuminated only by the reflected saffron glow of the London lights. The touch of body against body awakened a shivering ecstasy as they held each other with suffocating closeness, and a passion that swirled them to the heights of ecstasy. There was no tomorrow, only the present as she whispered, 'Oh *Ross*.' Her voice was husky, her yearning no less great because desire had been satiated.

He kissed her forehead, a smothered endearment escaping his lips as they lay there and lapsed into eloquent silence, their hold tightening spasmodically until at last she cried, 'You must go . . . Janet wants to talk to you . . . she is waiting.'

'It's unfair to you,' he murmured, 'but I couldn't stay away . . . I told you you'd bewitched me—'

She raised herself on one elbow and looked down into his face, her bare breast against his chest. As she kissed him his arms imprisoned her for a breathless second and then, sighing, he released her.

They stood together in the sitting room a little while later, their need lessened, but not assuaged. The sleep that follows fulfilment was denied them, and the thought of it was expressed in the deep gaze they exchanged as he said, 'This is a form of exquisite torture.' He leaned forward and kissed her forehead. 'But there's tomorrow,' he said in a low voice, adding, 'so until the morning, darling.'

They walked, arm-in-arm, to the front door; she drew her flimsy house-coat around her and tightened its sash before opening the door while concealing herself behind it. Their eyes met; their gaze deepening for a fraction of a second, and he was gone.

Had it been a dream? Anita asked herself as she returned to the bedroom. Yet the disarrayed duvet, the indented pillows, bore testimony to the truth. Her heart was still thumping; emotion making her feel light-headed and incapable of rational thought. If anyone had told her she could plunge into such a relationship, she would have thought them mad.

Yet here she was, so overwhelmed by the fascination of this man that his touch robbed her almost of sanity. It was like being at the mercy of a drug she craved above all else. *Ross*. She was not going to spoil the happiness and wonder of that past hour, by analysis. She had insisted on not wanting commitments at this stage; why dwell on their possibility, or try to speculate about tomorrow? But, later, before she fell asleep, the disturbing thoughts struck her: Why had Ross shown such tolerance over Kenneth, once the first flash of anger abated? Could he have an ulterior motive by way of accepting her friendship with Kenneth, on the tacit understanding that she, in turn, accepted his closely-knit relationship with Glynis, irrespective of the guardian/ward relationship? The possibility brought an element of suspense, tinged with faint suspicion.

Ross came down early from his flat the following morning and was already in his consulting room when Anita arrived.

'We couldn't have timed it better,' he said in greeting. 'No one in yet.'

They were intensely aware of each other, the spell of the previous evening lingering, excitement building up as their eyes met.

Anita deliberately tried to inject a note of humour, 'Your presence so early would make the Guinness Book of Records!'

'I had an incentive to be early.' With that he took her in his arms.

After a second or two she managed to struggle free.

'I'm here to work,' she reminded him, anxious to

maintain some control to which to cling during the day.

'Work for *me*,' he retorted, with a low throaty chuckle.

Anita said irrelevantly and urgently, 'You mentioned my coming to Wilmington for the weekend . . . Janet and Glynis may feel—'

His expression warned her against finishing the sentence.

'I invite whom I choose to Monk's Corner,' he said sharply. 'And they both like you. Of course, if you don't want to come—'

She both wanted to do so and, at the same time, was reluctant to follow her inclinations because of Glynis, whose reference to the weekend had seemed subtly to emphasise her own privileged position, there being more in what she didn't say than in a multitude of words.

'It isn't that,' she said.

'Then—what?' he demanded.

Her expression was unconsciously appealing. 'I need time to get my breath, Ross. Perhaps when next you all go down . . .'

He avoided her gaze as he agreed, 'Very well, then.'

Anita felt relieved but a little surprised. She had not expected such a swift conciliatory acceptance, and doubted the wisdom of her decision; a decision which, later, she had cause bitterly to regret.

The telephone rang on his private line, cutting into a silence that had become tense and strained. He leaned over his desk and picked up the receiver. '*Fleur*!' he exclaimed, with obvious pleasure, and then added immediately, 'something wrong?'

Anita was about to leave, but he made a gesture for her to stay as he sat down, resting his elbow on his desk, smiling and saying 'Splendid.' Then, 'Sunday lunch? . . . I've a much better idea. Why not come down to Monk's Corner with us on Friday—tomorrow? . . . Who's us? Why, Janet and Glynis, of course . . . You'd like to? Splendid. I could pick you up.' His laughter was infectious as he added, 'Very well, if you prefer to be independent . . . Whatever time suits you. I try to miss the rush hour; but I'll make a point of being early.' He laughed again. 'Goodbye . . . until tomorrow.' As he replaced the receiver the inter-com went. Glynis wanted to make sure he hadn't an 'emergency' with him.

'Come along in,' he said brightly. 'Anita's here.'

Glynis joined them, looking faintly suspicious.

'You're early,' she observed, trying not to sound critical.

He might not have heard her.

'I was speaking to Fleur just now,' he said. 'She's joining us tomorrow.'

'At Monk's Corner?' Glynis's voice rose slightly on a note almost of interrogation.

'Where else?'

'It's a long while since Fleur has been there.' Then, seeing the frown that puckered Ross's brows, she added hurriedly, 'Be fun.' She tried to inject a note of enthusiasm into her voice without succeeding, but Ross did not notice. He glanced at his watch and said, like a man clicking back into professional time, 'I'm due at the hospital . . .' He looked at Anita, 'Get on to Jennings about Mrs

Moore's X-rays . . . I want them here before I see her . . . I'll be back for Mrs Chard.'

'Who'll wait uncomplainingly,' Glynis said, and Anita could hear the edge in her voice.

With that Ross went out like someone disappearing into another world.

'So Fleur's in the picture again,' Glynis said as though the words were wrested from her.

'A very lovely—'

Anita wasn't able to finish the sentence. Glynis cut in, 'I just wanted us to have a weekend on our *own*!' It was the spoilt child talking; being petulantly indiscreet, then suddenly regaining control. 'What are *you* going to do this weekend?'

Anita gave a thoroughly uncharacteristic and rash reply, 'Probably seeing Kenneth . . . he won't be working *all* the hours.' The words came out before she had time to weigh up their significance. But there was a smarting sense of inadequacy churning within her. Fleur Sheriden's telephone call had crashed into her conversation with Ross, and while it would seem that they had settled the issue of her visit to Monk's Corner, she would like to have felt a greater degree of harmony and closeness. She had not sought persuasion but, womanlike, wanted her point of view fully understood. Nevertheless panic gripped her as she realised the folly of making such a random statement about her movements, since doubtless Glynis would repeat it.

'Fortunate your meeting Kenneth again.' Glynis managed subtly to convey that the benefit was all on Anita's side. 'Anyway, have fun. It must be pretty grim to be on one's own at the weekend.'

Anita made no comment, but crossed to the

desk, saying, 'If you'll excuse me I must see about those X-rays.'

Glynis gave a little smug smile and left.

Ross returned promptly to see his appointment patient. He studied Anita closely as he sat down at his desk. 'You know, a nurse's uniform wants a lot of beating when it comes to sex appeal,' he said unexpectedly. 'That ridiculous little cap suits you beautifully—'

'Because it is ridiculous!'

'No; because it seems a challenge!'

'Mrs Chard is here and you cannot afford to prolong the consultation,' Anita dared to say. 'Glynis will not be best pleased if you are late this evening.'

'I don't need reminding,' he said shortly.

'I'm sure you don't,' she flashed at him.

Emotion was whipping up anger which neither could manage to conceal.

Ross flicked down the inter-com. 'Mrs Chard,' he said briefly.

And for the rest of the day, he and Anita hardly had a minute in which to speak to each other. When the last appointment ended he said, 'I'm going up to shower and change.'

'You asked me to remind you that you have a consultation with Sir Robert Lang at Hampton Court, to see Mrs Greenway tomorrow morning.'

He made a gesture to suggest that it *had* slipped his memory. 'I shall have to allow for the traffic. Friday is a villainous day.' He paused, looked at her intently and was about to speak, then thought better of it.

'Your first patient is at one o'clock,' Anita

added. She wanted to mention Kenneth and her conversation with Glynis, but he had reached the door. The fact that he was taking Glynis out lay between them with dangerous implication.

'Have a good evening,' she managed to say brightly, as the door closed behind him.

When Glynis rang on the inter-com, Anita explained that Ross had gone up to his flat.

'Ah,' Glynis exclaimed, well pleased. 'When it comes to it, Ross never keeps me waiting on a special occasion.'

The words struck a chill at Anita's heart, making her feel empty and hollow, but she instinctively lifted her head a trifle higher and drew upon courage and dignity. Suppose Ross was annoyed because of her refusal to go to Monk's Corner? That was better than her being a clinging vine, agreeing to his every suggestion until she was taken for granted.

Ross returned to the consulting room half-an-hour later, already changed and immaculate in grey.

'Still here?' he sounded surprised.

Would he make any attempt to kiss her? Introduce a note of intimacy?

'Sterilising,' she said briefly.

'I left my credit card case in the drawer,' he explained. 'Absent-mindedly put them there! Heaven knows why.' His gaze rested upon her with a deep desirous look. Then he said abruptly, 'I'd better go.' He pocketed the sheaf of cards in their leather case. The tone of his voice brought the colour to her cheeks and she swiftly moved out of his path as he crossed to the door. Alone, she finished her tasks and was the last to leave. Mrs Baxter and Emily had gone promptly at five-thirty. The house seemed vast and empty, holding the faint smell of ether in its cool atmosphere. A secretary to one of the other consultants who rented rooms, came out of a door on the ground floor.

'We seem to be last,' she said, adding with a sigh, 'it's been one of those hellish days.' She was a dark, direct girl in her early thirties, who had been with her employer for ten years. She knew Anita had joined Ross recently and asked, 'How's it going?'

'Fine,' Anita said lightly.

'I only catch the occasional glimpse of Mr Charming. You're lucky!'

Anita had a sudden vision of herself in Ross's arms and felt that her thoughts must be noisy.

'Yes,' she murmured.

The door-bell rang, making Anita jump.

'Don't worry . . . it's most likely to be my boy-friend. He promised to pick me up.'

A pleasant-faced sporting type of young man stood on the steps. Anita smiled, said good-evening, and hurried away, feeling intensely lonely, almost bereft. The question racing through her mind brought jealousy and fear. Just what was Ross's relationship with Glynis? And how much longer could she, herself, remain in the dark?

CHAPTER SIX

FRIDAY hardly allowed Anita to have more than a few professional words with Ross who, returning from his Hampton Court patient, went from one consultation to another, with a steady stream of patients as was customary. But on this occasion a couple of 'Can you possibly fit her in?' cases—sent from their respective harrassed doctors—added to the work-load. Any hope of leaving early for Wilmington vanished in the mid afternoon. No mention was made of the previous evening, and as Glynis had taken the morning off while Ross was away, Anita and she had no opportunity for conversation. It did strike Anita, however, that Glynis was looking particularly starry-eyed, even a little mysterious. Fleur Sheriden telephoned during the morning, to re-cap on the route Ross took to Wilmington, and Anita was able to enlighten her.

'Ah, so you know Monk's Corner?' Fleur said brightly, her tone encouraging.

Anita explained that she had spent the weekend there, feeling a pang because she was not going that day.

'Then we may meet again sometime,' came the parting comment.

Anita had the distinct feeling that Fleur Sheriden was more than a little attracted to Ross; a fact that had registered on her professional visit.

Ross listened with interest as Anita relayed details of the call. It was at the end of the day, and he clipped his fountain-pen in his jacket with an air of finality. A door might have shut between them.

Anita watched from a point across the large lofty room, recalling his words about 'being mystified by her coming to work for him when she had so many options open'. Then, she had doubted if he would recognise her in the street. Now, he had the same detached manner—distant and impersonal. What was he thinking? Would he leave without a word, or striking one intimate note? What had happened the previous evening? She hesitated even to ask him about it and then, almost on a note of defiance, said, 'Did you enjoy the concert?'

He looked at her without betraying a flicker of emotion.

'Very much.' He got up from his chair, straightened himself, stood for an imperceptible second as though making sure he had not forgotten anything, then as he walked to the door said pointedly, 'I hope your weekend will come up to your expectations. Goodnight.'

Anita stood, heart racing; legs feeling like celery-sticks. '*Come up to your expectations*'. No words could have been more significant, or conveyed more graphically what was in his mind. Of course Glynis had told him about Kenneth. Fool—*fool* that she had been to salve her pride by mentioning his name. The weekend now stretched like a desert, and every nerve in her body was taut, almost painful. Ross would be at Monk's Corner, not only with Glynis, but with Fleur Sheriden, who obviously attracted him. What, after all, did she, Anita, know about him? That his reputation was good?

That he was considered charming, attractive, and a brilliant surgeon? She could prove those things, but it still left the man—the real *man* to be accounted for.

Mrs Baxter rang on the inter-com, 'Shall I—?'

Anita didn't wait for the end of the sentence. 'I'll lock up . . . have a good weekend,' she said, and inwardly shrieked at herself for using the worn-out trite phrase. 'A good weekend'! What, she demanded fiercely, was good about it?

She went out of the building a little later like a whirlwind, head held high, eyes filled with the light of battle, her steps swift and determined. Damn Ross Wyndham! After a few minutes she slowed down a little and breathed deeply. At least she had annoyed him, and he was obviously sufficiently interested to be affected by her behaviour! But that was probably on account of his conceit, and the fact that he was accustomed to adulation, his professional status also giving his every word authority and importance. Having thus indulged in wholly destructive criticism, she was pacified.

On Saturday morning she shopped in Marylebone High Street and bought a new dress, in the spirit of one eating chocolates for comfort, while telling herself that the dress would be very useful while she was with Janet at Monk's Corner. Ross had not mentioned the arrangement, probably because their time together had been so limited. Her thoughts became unruly. *Nurse Pettifer* . . . was she another one who had a crush on Ross?

The day dragged; she didn't feel like eating, and somewhat defiantly poured herself out a sherry, beginning idly to eat nuts as she sipped it. It was a hot spring day with the sun streaming in at the windows, reminding her of the cool green country-side, and the pool at Monk's Corner. A pang shot through her. If Glynis had told Ross that she was seeing Kenneth, then, in all fairness, Ross could only assume that the arrangement was responsible for her avoiding going to Wilmington. She felt hot and wretched at the likelihood, ashamed of her previous attitude. There was, she decided finally, nothing she could do about it except explain to him. A little of the gloom lifted, and she set about doing all the odd jobs neglected during the week, the radio on without her actually listening to it.

It was six o'clock when the door-bell rang, and while she knew it was impossible, Ross's name rushed to her lips. But Kenneth said, 'I came on the off-chance that you'd have something to eat with me. I'm off for a couple of hours.'

She was pleased to see him, despite herself. He was, after all, a link with the past and nothing could alter the fact that Ross was with Glynis and Fleur Sheriden. Why shouldn't she enjoy an hour or so of harmless companionship? Kenneth might flirt a little, but they understood each other.

'Come in,' she said brightly, and then stopped, arrested by the somewhat solemn, subdued expression on his face. 'Anything wrong?'

'Not really. I'm just fed up with *me*!'

'Heavens! Why?' She preceded him into the sitting room, indicated the drinks tray so that he could help himself, then sat down on the sofa, waiting for his reply.

'I bungle everything.'

'Certainly not professionally,' she insisted.

'Emotionally,' he said a trifle vehemently.

Anita retreated, not wanting any further post-mortem on their earlier relationship.

'We all bungle things emotionally! Whether it is true that we learn from our mistakes is another matter . . . I'll have a sherry,' she added swiftly.

He poured it out, helped himself to a whisky, and sat down beside her.

'I can't ever see you bungling things,' he said, his gaze steady and unnerving. 'There's an art in not becoming too involved. All the same, you have just something about you these days, as I said the other evening . . . not exactly sophistication, but rather bewitching, all the same.'

The word struck hard and made her thoughts of Ross almost visual.

'Nonsense!' she said with a laugh. 'Your imagination again. I'm a hard-working woman, don't forget. Your adjectives—' She paused, lowering her gaze.

He continued to assess her, his brows slightly puckered, 'And you look even more enchanting when you blush,' he added. 'I'm not flirting with you, Anita.' His voice was low and serious.

'Splendid,' she retorted, injecting a note of gaiety. 'Now, seriously, tell me your plans—if you have any. Self-deprecation won't get you anywhere.'

His steady scrutiny was unnerving, and she sensed an element of danger which made her tense and uneasy. The light-hearted companion vanished, and in his place came a determined, persistent pursuer, as he cried, 'You're everything any man could want: elusive, but tempting . . .

Anita—' He leaned towards her, taking her in his arms possessively and with determination as his lips sought hers.

She shrank back, 'No, Kenneth—'

'Why not? We're—'

'Friends, I hope,' she said firmly. 'I'm not in a flirting mood.'

'And I'm not *flirting*,' he retorted, voice raised. He added, almost as though the revelation was a shock to himself, 'I'm in love with you—don't you understand? In love with you,' he repeated, his tone almost bewildered.

'They're just words,' she insisted, wanting to escape from their inevitability. 'Kenneth, you and I—'

He cut in on a note of anger, 'Could put back the clock; go on *together* . . . so! You don't want to be tied . . . I'm ready—'

Anita moved slightly, intending to get to her feet, but he forestalled her, and drew her back into his arms, his kiss rough and passionate, his arms sliding over her body with a familiarity that made her cry out, and wrench herself free.

He straightened himself instantly, 'I'm sorry,' he murmured, 'forgive me. I've been struggling not to face the truth ever since I saw you again. I'd rather do anything than hurt you, or lose your good opinion of me.' He stood up as he spoke, looking down at her as she was straightening her dress and regaining some semblance of composure.

'Let's forget it,' she said, her tone crisp. The thought of Ross brought an overwhelming sensation of guilt, even though she had contributed nothing to the scene. Dismay touched her because she knew that she could not dismiss the incident, or ignore what had been said.

'I love you,' he said solemnly. 'It isn't any excuse, but—' He sighed deeply and flung out his hands in a despairing gesture. 'I told you I bungle things,' he finished, sitting down opposite her, his expression dejected, his manner slightly baffling, as a look of near-disgust crept into his eyes.

It suddenly seemed important to Anita not to lose his friendship, or to allow this episode to ruin their relationship. 'I've said, let's forget it,' she repeated, hurrying on, 'we're hardly strangers, Kenneth—'

'Your resistance seemed almost guilty.'

Anita forced a little laugh.

'I was surprised,' she admitted honestly.

'Are you in love with someone else?' The question was direct and inescapable.

'No,' she replied. 'I've never really been in love, as they term it. There are so many degrees of emotion—all confusing.'

'You can say that again,' he retorted ruefully, and leaning forward kissed her gently on the forehead. 'I have no doubt whatsoever about my love for you,' he said seriously. 'If only I'd realised it in the past. Damn fool!' he finished vehemently.

'Kenneth—'

'What?' His voice was eager.

'Don't have any illusions.'

He looked at her reflectively. 'Hope is given to us all. Life is complicated enough without being deprived of that.'

Anita made no comment. She was thinking of Ross, and how impossible it was to understand, or even assess, her feelings for him, or his for her.

Kenneth darted a glance at his wrist-watch.

'The time!' he exclaimed. 'It would have to be a very hurried meal.'

'I'll do bacon and eggs—mushrooms; and I have sausages,' she suggested, and again felt that Ross was standing beside her, his expression like thunder.

'That would be perfect, if it isn't too much trouble.'

Anita regretted the offer almost immediately, not because of any work involved, but because it stamped a certain intimacy on the scene. But she knew beyond all doubt that Kenneth would not attempt to make love to her again, and that his general behaviour would be impeccable.

When the meal was over, he sat back in his chair and said, 'A banquet! I've only had a piece of toast and a cup of cold tea so far today. There was a pile-up near us, and we had to work flat out . . . Thank you,' he added quietly, and there was gratitude in his expression which had very little to do with the actual food.

When he was about to leave he asked, 'Will you be going to Monk's Corner next weekend?' There was a note of anxiety in the question.

'I very much doubt it.'

'Because you are not keen to go?' He looked at her steadily.

'Because my plans are uncertain . . . why? Will you be going?'

'Most probably. I've an open invitation and it's a marvellous break. Come, Anita.' He was persuasive.

'No promises,' she said firmly.

He stood for a second, contemplating her almost with an air of sadness about him. Then, 'Thank you for being you,' he said, and hurried to his car.

Anita shut the front door and went slowly back to the small dining area, separated from the kitchen by an archway. She cleared the table and washed up mechanically. The evening had been unexpected, and left her with a faint sense of shock. Everything around her seemed to be reaching a climax, even though she had no idea what form it would take. The pleasant, semi-familiar relationship she had previously enjoyed with Kenneth would inevitably change now that she knew he was in love with her. But, at least, she had salvaged a semblance of friendship which seemed vitally important to her. Was Kenneth an antidote for Ross? She put the knives and forks in their drawer and shut it with determination. Leave tomorrow to look after itself.

Despite this resolution, Anita felt a certain trepidation when confronting Ross after the weekend. His manner was politely distant, as on the previous Friday, but he enthused about the weekend, commenting on the perfect weather and that they had gone to the Theatre Royal in Brighton. Anita made suitable remarks, but maintained silence so far as her own activities were concerned. The beginning of the week was not the time to bring up matters of dissention, and when eventually she did discuss Kenneth, she wanted to be coherent and not at a disadvantage. But Ross said unexpectedly and abruptly, 'I notice your reluctance to mention *your* weekend. Did it come up to your expectations?'

'I hadn't any "expectations",' she countered.

'Oh, come now,' he protested, 'you wouldn't have declined to join us unless you had very good reason.'

Anita exclaimed with emphasis, 'I declined to join you because I thought it discreet to do so. I don't want either Janet or Glynis to think that I am—' She hesitated.

'What?' he demanded.

'Taking advantage; pushing myself, if you like.'

'Nonsense! And I detest feeble excuses. There was no reason why you shouldn't have said you were seeing Kenneth.'

'There was every reason, since I was *not* seeing him.'

Ross's mouth hardened. 'Then why tell Glynis that you were?' He hurried on, 'She merely mentioned it in passing because she was sorry you weren't coming down.'

Anita wanted to explode. Glynis wanted her company as much as a hole in her head!

'I simply mentioned that I *might* see him.'

'Don't play with words.'

'Then don't you either. I haven't the faintest idea why I mentioned the possibility of seeing Kenneth. I had absolutely no plans to do so.'

Ross looked at her as though she was under cross-examination. 'I find that difficult to believe.'

'Which proves the cliché that truth is stranger than fiction.'

Emotion was creeping insidiously between them; their awareness of each other reaching a dangerous crescendo.

'Then if that *is* so, you will not have seen him, I take it.'

The words struck like thunder in silence, echoing sinisterly.

Anita's heart was thumping and a sick sensation churned at the pit of her stomach. Ross's stare was merciless.

'Don't bother to lie to me, Anita. Of *course* you saw him. And I'm not for a moment disputing your right to do so; it is just that I dislike your methods. On the surface, this whole thing is trivial, but it strikes at the heart of any relationship. Why, in heaven's name, couldn't you have told me you were seeing him in the first place, instead of all this play-acting? It isn't a crime to prefer his company to mine.'

'I did not "prefer his company" to yours,' she cried angrily, helpless against an increasing feeling of inadequacy. She hated being the object of his wrath and contempt, and at the disadvantage of appearing deceptive. A little shiver went over her as she realised how, with a few harmless words, Glynis had subtly established her relationship with Kenneth as being of paramount importance.

The telephone rang on the private line. Ross answered it and said, in a somewhat surprised but friendly voice, 'Nurse Pettifer! How are you?'

Anita tensed. So! Already things had been set in motion for Janet's post-operative care. In which case, why couldn't Ross have mentioned it?

A few commonplace utterances followed until Ross said, 'This is quite a co-incidence . . .' There was a sudden pause before he added, 'Oh, now I understand; you've already been alerted. My ward thinks of everything. Splendid. And you are available? Yes, certainly three weeks. I don't believe in rushing things. I'm so grateful you can manage it, and that time is no stumbling block. Of course; just as soon as we know when the operation is to take place. It isn't an emergency from that point of view.'

When he replaced the receiver Ross said, 'One thing about Glynis: she doesn't waste any time in setting things in motion.'

Or, Anita thought, in taking the reins without Ross's authority. It emphasised her privileged position.

'I'm quite sure, in any case, that you'd find it simple to replace me at any time.' Anita's voice held a note of cynicism. She felt that she was sitting on a time-bomb, her emotions churned up; the prospect of the weeks ahead adding to her depression. She waited, tense, for his comment, wanting, despite herself, some sign of regret that they must be apart for an indefinite period.

'That, I am sure, would equally be true in reverse,' he replied coldly.

Glynis joined them at that moment.

'I forgot to tell you that Nurse Pettifer—'

Ross cut in, 'She has just telephoned.'

'Oh, good. I thought it wise to contact her, not knowing what her plans are these days.' She was studying Ross as she spoke, knowing that she had acted without his authority, but eager to prove that Anita was in no way indispensible.

Ross merely nodded his approval.

'Has Fleur rung?' Glynis rushed on.

Ross smiled. 'While I was in the shower.'

'She loved every minute of the weekend. You're going to the theatre, I hear. Let me know when, so that I can plan something, too.' She gave a little intimate laugh. 'You can't have it all your own way.'

To her annoyance Anita's heart felt that it was merely a weight in her body. She had no place in this conversation and it made her feel doubly an outsider. There was a moment's pause before Glynis went on, addressing Ross, 'By the way, Kenneth spoke to Janet this morning, adding his reassurance about the operation.'

Ross looked stony-faced.

Glynis turned to Anita, her smile warm and friendly. 'He mentioned that he'd seen you over the weekend and that you'd saved his life by cooking him a meal when he was starving . . . Perhaps you'll be able to come to Monk's Corner with him next weekend.'

Anita murmured her thanks, finding it impossible to judge Glynis's motives or moods.

Ross, coldly cynical, ignored the conversation as he said, 'I don't want Mrs Norman kept waiting. She is my first patient.'

The bell went at that juncture and Glynis moved to the door. 'Don't worry! I'm on my way, although it may not *be* your patient.' She disappeared, half-smiling.

Karen Norman came into the room a few minutes later. She was thirty-three, normally attractive, plump without being fat; child-like, but fiercely determined. Now she was breathless, her legs and ankles swollen, her cheeks highly-coloured. Ross's eyebrows went up in alarm as he saw her. She was a heart case—mitral stenosis—a narrowing of the mitral valve, causing the heart to work overtime in order to pump the blood through a narrow orifice, thus depleting the supply. Over the years Ross had fought many battles with her because she was desperately anxious to have a child, which was out of the question, since a pregnancy would endanger her life.

This time her attitude was different as she gasped with a kind of defiant delight, that nevertheless held a pathetic hint of fear, 'Now there's nothing you can say to me, Mr Wyndham. I'm going to have a baby—a baby,' she repeated with wonder.

Ross continued to study her in dismay, shocked by her general condition. Even her face was puffy and she looked ill.

'You were fitted with a coil,' he said, trying to conceal his disquiet.

'It came out,' she admitted, adding, 'I kept quiet about it, so that neither you, nor my doctor—Dr Lane—could do anything about it. My husband didn't know, and as he's away on business a great deal, he's just thought I'd put on a little weight.' She paused, and gasped for breath. 'No one is going to rob me of the baby—no one!'

Ross knew that, at this stage, he must humour her, encourage her to put him in the picture as much as possible.

'How long?'

'Six months.' Her eyes darted to his, silently pleading with him not to smash a dream.

'And how do you feel physically?' His voice was gentle and sympathetic. He knew the answer.

'I've been quite well,' she lied.

'"Been"?' he echoed promptingly, knowing she was not only trying to deceive him, but also herself.

She lowered her gaze. 'Well, you see, I'm . . . giddy; my head's bad, and now my husband's due back unexpectedly at the end of the week, having been away a month . . . he'll know . . . so I *had* to come to see you—' She broke off, hardly able to breathe, her cry for help anguished.

Ross's fears were growing. 'Let me take your blood pressure,' he said with some urgency, while wondering how he was going to deal with the situation he knew to be grave . . . 'No, don't move,' he added, drawing a chair to sit beside her, and taking the sphygmomanometer from Anita as she handed it to him. Later, he told himself, he would get Mrs Norman to the examining-couch and compare the pressure while at rest.

But at that moment Karen Norman gave a shudder and thudded from her chair to the floor in a fit due to pre-eclampic toxaemia—a fit epileptiform in character, because of abnormally high blood pressure and damage to her kidneys.

Ross, kneeling beside her and thrusting a handkerchief between her lips to prevent her biting her tongue, called to Anita, 'Dial 999 for an ambulance—quicker than hospital.' The look he flashed said, 'She could die at any moment'. Karen Norman was now unconscious.

Anita obeyed automatically. The call was made, giving name, condition of patient, address.

'You take over here,' Ross said urgently, 'while I arrange with St Mark's.' He got through to the Admission Medical Officer, stating the facts and adding, 'Tell my registrar to get a bed . . . Who's

the consultant gynaecologist on duty? . . . Mr
Gordon. Good.'

Within an incredibly short while the ambulance
men arrived and the patient was taken away.

There was a hush in the consulting room as Ross
and Anita faced each other. Ross sat down heavily
at his desk; Anita perched herself on the edge of a
chair.

'Is there any hope?' she asked.

'There are sometimes miracles,' he said, and
sighed doubtfully.

'The child?'

He shook his head. 'Now I understand why she
cancelled her previous appointment—something
about a cold.' He got up and paced the room. 'I
must contact Dr Lane . . . then there's the husband.' Ross was thinking aloud, looking at his
watch every now and then, as though time would
provide inspiration.

The inter-com went. The next patient was
waiting.

Then the telephone rang. It was Ross's registrar.

'Yes, William . . . Well?' Ross's voice was
clipped with anxiety.

Only a few words were spoken, but when Ross
replaced the receiver he looked at Anita and said,
'Mrs Norman died a matter of minutes after being
admitted.'

Anita just stared at him, too shocked to speak.
The silence was heavy and oppressive.

Ross flicked down the inter-com. 'Bring in the
next patient,' he said as though clinging to a life-
line, not daring to weaken or betray his emotions.

Anita looked at him, but she might not have been

there. No recognition flickered in his eyes, and she went swiftly into the examining-room, choking back the sobs that tore at her in sudden overwhelming unhappiness.

CHAPTER SEVEN

JANET'S operation was arranged for the second week in June, and Anita faced the prospect of its aftermath with foreboding. Ross's attitude in the meantime had been distantly polite with occasional lapses into friendliness, but without any hint of their former intimacy. In fact as Anita looked at him, it seemed impossible to believe that they had ever lain in each other's arms, or experienced a shared ecstasy. Obviously he had convinced himself that she preferred Kenneth, and had made feeble excuses over the weekend for that reason. She knew Ross to be a proud man who would never plead for favours, or tolerate deception, and it was impossible to extricate herself from the invidious position in which, foolishly, she had placed herself. Kenneth's avowed love for her seemed to add weight to the difficulties of the situation.

Janet went into St Mark's on the Sunday evening prior to the operation on the Monday. She hadn't the faintest idea what to expect and had not been a hospital patient for ten years, when she'd had an emergency appendectomy. The change in routine, the relaxing of rules, made the present day admission rather like taking up residence in a pleasant hotel. She had her own bathroom, and even a small refrigerator should she wish, or be allowed, any iced or alcoholic drinks.

Martin Jayson had been quietly confident and,

like most patients with their particular specialist, Janet had placed him on a pedestal, feeling that so long as she was in his hands on the operating table, all would be well. The thought uppermost in her mind was to be as little trouble as possible to the staff who, she knew, were always overworked.

'I want Anita to see you in,' Ross said firmly on the previous Saturday.

'I can see myself in,' Janet protested, while appreciating the thought.

'You will do nothing of the sort,' he insisted.

Janet smiled.

'Whatever is least worry,' she agreed, knowing that it was impossible to convey how adjusted she had become to the event. She reflected on how gentle Ross was in his concern for her, and how the medical profession in general reacted precisely as the laymen when it came to family involvements. They might completely ignore the *symptoms*, but when something specific was diagnosed, they were endearingly alarmed while pretending to be unconcerned!

'I must remind you that the operation is nothing,' she emphasised. 'So why the fuss?'

'There are the same procedures with every operation,' he reminded her. 'Don't argue! Just do as you're told!' He paused. 'You like Anita, don't you?'

'More than like her. Don't you?'

There was a sudden electric silence.

'She is my nurse,' he said somewhat stiffly.

'That is not what I meant—I mean, as a *person*. You've been very off-hand with her lately, I've noticed.'

'And you have a vivid imagination,' he warned her. 'Glynis would take you in—' he hurried on, 'but it is better to have someone—' He hesitated, his expression changing to that of authority, 'But Glynis and I will look in before dinner. You'll be having various tests before the operation.'

'Such as?'

'Blood, urine; electro-cardiogram; chest X-rays—the anaesthetist will see you, as well as a member of Martin Jayson's firm.'

'Uncle Tom Cobley and all, in fact. Ah well, I shan't be going anywhere!' Her mood changed. 'You'll keep an eye on Glynis,' she said suddenly. 'I mean . . . she'll be alone at the flat, and while she talks as though she's capable and independent, she needs—'

'Protection,' Ross cut in quietly. 'You can safely leave Glynis to me, so don't have any worries on that score. We shall be together most of the time, in any case.'

'With you in charge, I shan't worry,' Janet said, reassured. 'You have to remember that you are her . . . well . . . her *life* as it were.'

'I know that, too,' he said gravely.

'She has seemed rather distracted recently,' Janet said, seizing the opportunity to discuss the issue.

'I haven't noticed it,' Ross replied, while immediately alerted.

Janet smiled. 'Men are hardly the most observant creatures! I sometimes think that they would not notice if a woman developed two heads, so long as she was *there*!'

'Utter libel,' he countered. 'I notice everything

about Glynis! After all, she is my—my—' He hesitated, and added swiftly, 'My ward. Why should she be distracted?'

Janet plunged, 'Perhaps because you, too, seem to be afflicted by the complaint lately.'

Ross didn't lower his gaze.

'And you have X-ray eyes, cataract or no cataract!'

'Wait until I can see properly!' she warned him.

'I've had a lot on my mind,' he admitted. 'Life can sometimes get complicated, and timing is very important.'

Janet asked herself if he was thinking of marriage to Glynis, and wondered why an engagement hadn't materialised before now. She had expected the announcement to be made upon Glynis's return from her holiday earlier in the year, since it had always been regarded as a foregone conclusion. She recalled the first evening that she and Glynis had met Anita—Glynis's resentment of her, and opposition to mixing 'business with pleasure'. Was she now jealous of Anita? The possibility was disturbing. Janet could not forget her own assessment that Glynis had a malicious streak. Was Anita in any way, even indirectly, responsible for this somewhat turbulent state of affairs? When it came to it, Janet reflected, Anita, too, had been very subdued and much to her surprise, had declined invitations to the cottage. Kenneth, too, her thoughts raced on, had not been his usual ebullient self. Why, she asked somewhat desperately, think of all these disturbing thoughts now? Of course Ross had a lot on his mind; his work was demanding and exacting.

St Mark's, however, seemed to be a panacea when she and Anita arrived there that Sunday morning and were shown into her room by a cheery-faced nurse, with large blue eyes and a welcoming smile.

'I'd undress and get into bed,' she suggested. 'We'll want to take your blood pressure, etcetera, and there's no reason why you shouldn't have a rest!' She shot Janet a look of assessment, judging her to be one of the good patients who wouldn't cause any trouble, and would do as she was told without fuss or complaint.

Anita shut the door and looked around her. It was a fair-sized room with two arm-chairs and two small ones; the usual sliding bed-table, locker, chest-of-drawers, wardrobe. A panel of bells, telephone and light switches was beside the bed. The cream-shaded walls and patterned blue-and-gold curtains escaped austerity.

'I'll unpack, while you undress,' Anita said cheerfully, 'then I can put your things away.'

Janet sat down on the edge of the bed; she felt suddenly helpless and childish as though taken over by remote control. It wasn't an unpleasant feeling as she realised that for the next five days she would be under surveillance.

'I feel like a race-horse under starter's orders,' she said with a little laugh. 'I think I'll rather enjoy not having to think, or make decisions, for a while!'

'Hospitalisation is an "out of the world" experience,' Anita said with a smile. 'Everyone wants to "come out" as quickly as possible, and yet feels a pang at leaving the absolute security behind. You, at least, haven't any home worries, or crying children left behind.' As she spoke she began to unpack what seemed to be an inordinate number of nightdresses.

'I hate being short of things,' Janet said half-apologetically.

'Don't worry! You won't be,' Anita chuckled, and with expert organisation put away everything speedily but calmly.

Janet climbed into bed and settled herself on the pillowed bed-rest.

'Staff' in her blue uniform, pert little cap and red belt came in, looking approvingly at Janet.

'Good! Much better in bed. I want to take your blood pressure and pulse, and ask you a few questions.' She began filling in a chart which when completed was attached to Janet's bed.

Coffee and biscuits were brought immediately afterwards, with a cup for Anita. A menu, also, for lunch and supper on Sundays, from which Janet made her choice. Then she and Anita drank their coffee, Anita sitting in an arm-chair beside the long large windows that gave a view over streets and roof-tops. The noise of traffic was muted because the building lay back from the actual road. It suddenly became a strange isolated world.

'Will they bandage both my eyes?' Janet asked suddenly.

'No; only the operated eye. At one time it was an ordeal of three weeks flat on your back, your neck and head packed with sand-bags.'

Janet said, 'I'm terribly ignorant and I'm afraid I didn't really take in what Mr Jayson told me!' She looked at Anita and said irrelevantly, 'Are you feeling all right?'

Anita tensed. 'Of course. Why?'

'You look pale and—and solemn.'

'I'd rather be taking you to the theatre,' Anita laughed, 'than bringing you here!' She hastened, knowing that to be a foolish remark, 'Oh, don't misunderstand me—'

'I know what you mean; no alarm bells sounding, I assure you! But you haven't looked well lately.'

'Heat,' Anita said quickly. 'I love it better than it loves me. And it has been a particularly busy time.'

'True. Ross has been nervy.' Janet added hopefully, 'Perhaps a rest at Monk's Corner will do you good. I'm sure I shan't be too much of a nuisance. I'll certainly try not to be.'

Sister-in-charge came in at that moment.

'I'm sorry not to have been here to welcome you,' she apologised to Janet. 'The inevitable emergency. You're comfortable?'

Janet introduced Anita who studied Sister with appraisal. A tall statuesque woman of thirty-five with an excellent complexion and natural colour. She appeared to have all the time in the world and brought an atmosphere of authority and reassurance.

Janet said, with a half-apologetic smile, 'What *is* a cataract, Sister? I've been told, but I don't remember!'

Sister gave a little laugh. 'The lens of the eye, which is like a crystal-clear lozenge just behind the iris and black pupil, tends to change its chemical composition. Cloudy or opaque patches develop, which may grow slowly for several years; or the lens may become opaque within a few months.'

'So that's why, in the early stages, one gets

blurred sight; fuzzy print and bright lights?'

'Exactly; and as the cataract grows, so the sight goes. The operation enables the surgeon to remove the capsule and the lens,' Sister added, not going into minute details. 'Something in the region of fifty thousand cataracts were removed last year. All ages, though mostly over sixty,' Sister finished optimistically.

'I'll be sixty in August,' Janet volunteered.

'You'll be thrilled really to see again,' Sister said encouragingly. 'And you look much younger than sixty . . . "Staff" has seen you . . . Mr Wyndham's registrar spoke to me this morning and I understand Mr Wyndham will be here this evening.' She looked pleased. 'I know Mr Wyndham,' she said as though the fact was enough. Obviously Ross was a favourite.

Anita sat there, aching with a sense of loss because she and Ross were not intimately associated any more. Their relationship had, she thought desolately, been bizarre.

To her amazement Ross came into the room at that moment.

Sister looked delighted, her greeting spontaneously welcoming, with just a touch of deference.

'I had to come in to visit a patient,' Ross explained. 'Thought I'd take a look at you. I see we've got her in bed, Sister? Splendid. Keep her in order.'

Janet laughed.

'You're talking as though I were a child,' she protested.

'Which is what all patients are,' Ross insisted. 'Eh, Sister?'

Sister was thinking how handsome Ross looked. It took a great deal for her to notice any consultant, she would freely admit, but Ross was different.

'Indeed, Mr Wyndham. And some of them are naughty children, too!'

'Pity we can't open a bottle of champagne,' Ross said brightly.

'Shall I be allowed a sherry afterwards?' Janet asked.

'By the time you leave—certainly,' Sister promised. She glanced down at the watch pinned to her bosom. 'If you need anything, Mrs Wyndham . . .' She indicated the bell.

Anita looked at Ross and their gaze lingered as a wave of emotion flowed between them, making them aware of each other as though they were alone in the room. It was the first note of intimacy that had been struck for weeks, and Anita's heart felt that it had stopped beating for a second, only to start thumping heavily. Why, she thought fiercely, couldn't she resist him? Why should a look from him turn her world upside-down and wipe out all thought of her surroundings, making her long to be in his arms?

Janet wriggled her slim body in the bed with increasing satisfaction.

'Thank you,' she said gratefully to Sister. 'And for explaining about a cataract. This time I must remember, or Mr Jayson will think I'm mad.'

'I shouldn't worry,' Sister nodded. 'Very few people remember, when it really comes to it—'

'Except,' Anita managed to say in order to drag herself back to normality, 'those who talk of nothing but "my operation"!'

Sister laughed and went to the door. 'How right!'

Silence fell after she had gone. Ross sat down by the bed, looked around him and said, 'You'll be comfortable here.' He had the air of one who was completely at home. This was an integral part of his world and there was no doubting the authority and power he wielded. 'I've told William to look in on you,' he added.

'No rules and regulations,' Janet exclaimed.

'Not really.' He avoided looking at Anita.

'Where's Glynis?' Janet asked in the moment of awkward silence that fell.

'At the flat I imagine! You only left her a short while ago. She's coming to lunch with me at one-thirty. We'll be in this evening.'

'You don't need—'

'We'll be in this evening,' he insisted. 'But I must go now. I've to see a patient.'

'Today?' Janet sounded surprised.

'That's the worst of living over the shop,' he said, shooting Anita a swift glance. 'Mrs Tregrain.'

Anita remembered Mrs Tregrain whose lover had deserted her, and who had decided to try again to salvage something of her marriage. Was that failing again?

'You could write a column in a woman's maga-zine,' Anita said, 'hints to husbands.'

Ross countered, 'Or lovers.' He got to his feet, looking down at Janet with deep affection, thinking of all the help, consideration and love she had given him, and his father, over the years. It didn't matter how trivial the operation, the very fact of it touched his heart in a way totally unexpected. A protective, filial emotion overwhelmed him. He put a hand on her shoulder and kissed her cheek.

'I'll be back,' he said, and hurried from the room.

And while Anita was not lost to the significance of the scene, all she could hear was the echo of his words, 'Or to lovers'. What had lain behind the remark? The regret at ever having become *her* lover? Was that the message implicit in the words?

'I'll just make sure everything is in order in the bathroom,' Anita said, feeling claustrophobic as she sat there, imagining her thoughts to be visual and aware that Janet was studying her with more than usual intensity, probably due to the circumstances and the solitude of the moment.

'Sponge-bag; tooth-brush, paste; talc,' she said aloud from the adjoining room. 'We haven't forgotten anything. The Guerlain Mitsouko *eau de toilette* spray is luxurious. The nurses will love the scent of that!' She returned to the bedroom, admiring Janet's delicate pink lacy nightdress with matching jacket. A warm appreciation and affection for her surged, and just then she seemed so much a part of Ross—involved and representative.

'Now you must go,' Janet said with concern. 'This will have taken up your entire morning by the time you get back to your flat.'

A knock came at the door and William March, Ross's registrar, appeared.

'Any admittance? The Big White Chief has already been in, I understand.' He shook Janet's hand and nodded to Anita. She had met him the previous week.

'News travels fast in hospital corridors,' Anita said with a laugh.

'A day ahead of the *Daily Mail!* Everything satisfactory?' He studied Janet as he spoke.

'I feel like Exhibit A,' Janet laughed.

'They'll wheel you to X-ray for the chest, and the cardiac department for the electrocardiogram.'

'Why can't I walk?'

'Because we make a fuss of our patients,' he said with a smile. He was a tall, athletic man with reddish fair hair and a wide generous mouth. The kind of man, Anita thought, she would like as a brother.

'So I'm beginning to appreciate . . . It's very much a fantasy world; unreal,' Janet exclaimed, looking around her. 'Now you *must* be going, Anita . . . I feel guilty.'

'Don't! I'll be in on Tuesday. No visitors on op days.'

'Because I'll still be whoosy?'

'Yes; probably.' Anita didn't add that she would also have to lie flat on her back immediately after the operation and during the first night.

Janet nodded. 'People don't remember much about coming round,' she said reflectively, recalling her previous experience.

'Cases, and patients, vary,' William said cautiously.

'Anita's taking me to Monk's Corner at the end of the week. I shall go straight from here,' Janet explained. 'Oh, just stopping at the flat to collect a few things.'

'Splendid . . . now I must get back to work.' He went from the room, white coat flapping.

'Kenneth's coming to see me on Tuesday,' Janet said irrelevantly. 'We haven't seen very much of him just lately. But he keeps in touch.' Her gaze focussed on Anita half-expectantly.

But Anita did not pursue the conversation. She left a few minutes later just as lunch was about to be served. As she walked down the long corridor towards the lift, she felt the pulse of a big hospital beating dramatically. The smell of ether and disinfectant hung in the air nostalgically. Why shouldn't she return to this life? Leave Ross. Nurse Pettifer might be only too glad to take over her job permanently. Absent-minded, she walked past the lifts for that particular floor, her thoughts absorbed wholly with the remembrance of the look Ross had given her; the look they had exchanged as though the world around them had vanished, making it yesterday. If they could recapture *that* degree of emotion, why not be able to bridge the recent gulf? Her nerves tingled, her body heated, and at that moment she ran out of corridor, standing lost by an emergency staircase. Disgusted with herself, she retraced her steps, took the large empty lift and went out into bright hot summer day, leaving the gaunt grey building behind her; but not before she had thought of all the suffering it represented—and the healing. Just for a second, Janet seemed a lonely figure.

To her amazement a voice at her elbow said, 'I came here on the off-chance, and saw your car parked nearby. I've been to the Middlesex.'

'Kenneth!' He filled the emptiness of the day ahead.

'No chance of having lunch with me at the Doctor's Restaurant near Mortimer Street?'

What, she asked herself, had she to lose? Anything would be better than her own company, and that did not deprecate the invitation.

'I'd even like the *patient's* restaurant!'

Kenneth hastened, 'I know Janet has gone in. I spoke to her this morning and she told me, as she put it, that you were "going to deliver the parcel"! She's all right?'

'Fine . . . What do we do with two cars?'

'Drive our own. You follow me! Ross is still here, I notice—his car's over there on the consultants' park.'

Anita had been so absorbed by her thoughts of him that she had forgotten what he said about visiting a patient. Would *he* have noticed Kenneth's car? The possibility was remote, she consoled herself, unless Kenneth had been there quite a time. She asked him if he'd been waiting long, to which he replied, to her relief, 'Only about ten minutes.' She ridiculed herself for worrying about the matter, arguing that it would, also, be too much of a co-incidence. Nevertheless she had the uncanny feeling that Ross's ghost was watching her from the hospital steps.

'Would you marry me?' Kenneth asked her over lunch, 'assuming you were prepared to face up to commitments after all?' He paused. 'That's badly put. I mean . . . would I have a chance, all things being equal?' He hung on her reply.

Anita looked at him very levelly. 'I can't answer hypothetical questions about hypothetical situations, Kenneth. I have no thoughts whatsoever about marriage at the moment.'

He sighed and shrugged his shoulders. 'Fair enough,' he agreed. 'I suppose it's that damned elusive quality about you that's so maddening.'

'Life's a contrary business,' she murmured. It struck her that she had never mentioned Ross and Glynis to him, nor, even by inference, referred to their relationship.

The words came with sudden irrelevance, 'What do you think about Ross and Glynis?' The question was so unexpected that Kenneth exclaimed almost with clipped guardedness.

'I don't follow. I should have thought it was self-evident.'

'Their being guardian and ward?' It wasn't what Anita wanted to say, but the atmosphere made her self-conscious, almost as though she had been guilty of a *faux pas*.

'Of course.'

Something in his manner made her uneasy. Was he in a position of confidence, and knew the truth about Ross and Glynis' future? Anita changed the subject and made reference to Nurse Pettifer.

'Oh, yes,' Kenneth said with enthusiasm, 'Gillian Pettifer. Know her well. In fact I introduced her to Ross in the first place.' Kenneth gave an indulgent smile. 'She's always had an outsize crush on Ross. Whether or not he ever suspected it, and that was why he didn't take her on permanently, I wouldn't know.' He paused. 'One never does quite know with Ross. He and I have been good friends for some years, but I'd not dream of questioning him about his personal life.' He corrected that, ' "Questioning" is not the right word. I should say "prying". He's a very private kind of person. At the moment he's damned overworked; edgy. I make myself a bit scarce on these occasions.'

Anita felt that a cold hand had clutched her heart. Nurse Pettifer loomed large on the horizon. The question shot through her mind: Had Ross made love to her? The thought seemed an outrage. But why? Was she, Anita, so special? Could his behaviour be said to justify the claim? And didn't she, in her heart, want to be? What she found hardest to endure was the suspense, and her own inability completely to break away from his attraction and influence. A look from him and willpower vanished.

'That is what friendship is all about,' Anita commented with a sigh. 'You *will* come to Monk's Corner while I am there—I mean, with Ross and Glynis?'

'Oh, yes,' he replied immediately, adding with a certain defiance, 'On my own if needs be! Our "just good friends" relationship is well established.'

Anita felt uneasy, and again thought of Ross with trepidation.

'Why do relationships have to be catalogued?' Anita's inflection betrayed frustration.

'Because people like labels—everything neatly explained away. They suspect emotional hide-and-seek . . . You are beautiful, Anita. Your skin is so smooth and always looks cool—not a greasy mess!'

Anita laughed, nevertheless she found his intent gaze disconcerting. His manner changed as though he had some hidden grievance.

'I'm afraid I'll have to be going.' He spoke jerkily. 'I'm playing truant as it is.' He paid the bill and they went out into the almost deserted London streets, which had the strange hush of Sunday upon them.

'I'll be seeing you,' he exclaimed, before they drove away in their respective cars, each travelling in a different world. Anita asked herself if, after all, she was destined to marry Kenneth whose love, despite herself, she found a palliative. To fritter her life away, disdaining marriage and children, merely because Ross's arms offered her excitement and the ecstasy of sexual and sensual fulfilment, would be madness.

Janet was operated on at two o'clock the following day; sedated in bed and awakening only when it was all over. Her immediate reaction was of a slight pricking and soreness in the eye, otherwise she was drowsily content to return to sleep. She had an impression of muted light, soothing voices, and the imagery of post-anaesthetic illusion when her body seemed to be suspended in space.

To her delight the following morning she was allowed to go to the lavatory, admonished that she must not bend her head down, or bend over; or pick anything up from the floor. A somewhat difficult task when such movements came naturally. The bandaged eye was held with straps to her cheek, but she could see well with her left eye, so there was no problem. She was not allowed to bath, but given a blanket-bath instead. Her legs felt like cotton wool; she was empty, and still floating in a slightly unreal world.

Sister Holden came in when Janet was once more sitting up in bed.

'No pain?' she asked.

'None.'

'I'm going to have a look at you and put some

drops in your eye.' She lowered the bandage. The drops stung, but no more than that. Janet would like to have seen the eye, but was not given any opportunity.

Martin Jayson visited her later in the morning, expressed satisfaction, his soothing presence and cheerful manner inspiring confidence and giving reassurance. They joked a little and when he left, Janet's spirits could not have been higher, the fact that no physical ills were involved, contributing to her well-being.

Flowers began arriving from friends and even from Ross's patients, representing their tribute to him by way of concern for his step-mother. Some of the floral baskets were works of art, and much appreciated by the staff who were spared having to find vases to hold the blooms!

'Like a florist's shop,' Staff said admiringly. 'And the scent is marvellous.' She added, 'You can have your coffee out of bed.' Her voice came sharply, '*No*; don't lower your head!'

'Sorry.' Janet put a hand under her chin. 'One needs a permanent stiff neck for this. Or a splint.'

'I know.' The words were understanding, 'But you must remember , . . particularly when you try to put your slippers on.'

'Remote control,' Janet said, amused. 'Why these precautions?'

'Because bending over, or lifting anything heavy, increases the fluid pressure in the eye and puts a strain on the wounds.'

'A strange mysterious world,' Janet said wonderingly. 'Delicate surgery.'

'Very . . . Ah, Nurse,' as a familiar face appeared, 'we'll get Mrs Wyndham up!'

'And *we'll* be very good and not jerk *our* head about,' Janet grinned, sliding out of bed, head erect and feet groping for her slippers. 'It's like going back to the nursery—very cosy, with a lot of spoiling . . . How do you keep so cheerful and pleasant? Nurses really are wonderful.'

'Not always,' came the emphatic reply, on the edge of laughter. 'It depends on the patients.'

'And the boy friends,' Janet suggested.

'You can say that again,' came the fervent retort.

One or two people looked in later that morning and Janet found that the hours passed in a haze of unreality where thought seemed suspended. Glynis arrived immediately after lunch, saying that Ross would be there around six. Anita telephoned and said that she would wait until the following day, concerned that Janet should not be overtired.

When Anita arrived on that Wednesday evening, somewhat to her dismay she found Ross and Glynis already there.

'I thought I might be first,' she said half-apologetically, understanding that Ross had a consultation at a colleague's rooms in Weymouth Street.

'The more the merrier,' Janet said brightly. 'I had the bandage off for two hours this afternoon,' she rushed on, 'and I was examined again in Martin Jayson's "theatre"!' She laughed. 'A very dark room, full of equipment I don't understand. I only see shapes and images, but it is fascinating after not seeing *anything* out of that eye . . .'

Anita was listening, but aware of Ross's gaze

upon her, almost as though, in the company of other people, he dropped his guard and betrayed emotion.

Glynis said suddenly, 'Has Kenneth been in?' And while she glanced at Janet, she flashed Anita a half-inquiring gaze.

'Yes; before lunch today. He talked of joining us this evening, just for ten minutes.'

Kenneth's name immediately had significance and Anita saw Ross's mouth harden.

Naturally and deliberately she exclaimed, 'I ran into him when I left here on Sunday, by the way; we had lunch together at the Doctor's Restaurant somewhere near Mortimer Street.' If Kenneth, she reasoned, should happen to mention the fact, *now* Ross could hardly accuse her of deception! She looked at him with a bold defiance and saw anger and cynicism flash into his dark eyes. She also knew with faint trepidation that Glynis intercepted that look.

Anita seemed to be counting the hours as they ticked away, bringing her nearer to the moment when she would leave Ross and Harley Street. Nurse Pettifer came in on the Thursday morning to pick up the threads of the job, while Anita was there; and Anita, studying her, could see the wisdom of Kenneth's opinion.

'My grandfather left me some money,' she told Anita, 'so I am able to please myself whether I work or not. I don't have to do so; but coming here, to Mr Wyndham, is well—' she gave a little embarrassed nervous laugh, 'well, it isn't *like* work.'

She was attractive; with a friendly, cheerful

manner and even temper. Just, Anita thought, the kind of person Ross would appreciate. The thought did not console her. She wished she could have been plain and dowdy! Presentiment made Anita shiver: would she, herself, ever return to that Harley Street house?

When the time came to finish at the end of the day, and Nurse Pettifer had left, Anita lingered, knowing that she and Ross were alone in the house, apart from Mrs Smithers. It was a consoling thought, giving her a kind of priority. In those moments she felt that the world was theirs, their identity one.

'I don't think we've overlooked anything,' she said tensely.

'I wish I could come with you to collect Janet.' His sigh was deep. 'But operations won't wait.'

'I think it is as well for me to take Janet quietly down to Wilmington. Being in hospital is one thing; the world will look very strange to begin with. It's early days, after all.'

'You're right, of course. The arrangement couldn't be better . . . I want Glynis here to-morrow; we can't afford to be minus you *and* our receptionist.'

'You will have Nurse Pettifer.'

'Change is always strange,' he said briefly. 'I don't like it.'

Tension crept into the atmosphere. The evening sun threw a beam of light across the room, in which particles of dust danced like crumbled cobwebs, reminding them that the day was ending and that all sound in the house had stopped, leaving a silence that seemed to be listening dramatically.

Anita moved to the door.

He stood there, and it was as though some secret force was pulling his heart to hers as he cried, 'My God, I shall miss you!'

CHAPTER EIGHT

ANITA stood transfixed, hardly daring to breathe in case she had imagined the words. But he moved to her side and drew her almost roughly into his arms, his kiss deep, passionate and demanding. She responded in a convulsive turbulent need.

Then, abruptly, he released her. 'I'll see you over the weekend,' he murmured hoarsely.

Anita stumbled away, lost to her surroundings, seemingly blinded by emotion. Ecstasy, bewilderment, a flame of anger, touched her. Why had he remained silent after his tempestuous outburst? What did, 'I'll see you over the weekend', mean to convey in that context? And why, *why* hadn't she asked him? Turmoil, conflict and suspense, increased. Later, she looked back at the house as she walked away; it caught, and held, the atmosphere that had built up since she first entered it, as though it represented a record of all that had taken place within its four walls. The imposing façade and large windows; the solid Georgian walls were like a photograph signed by history. And she knew that some part of her would always remain there, no matter what the years ahead might bring.

Suddenly the struggle ended. '*My God, I shall miss you!*' The words echoed like music, and she intended to allow them to ring hopefully in her heart until she saw him again.

Martin Jayson saw Janet and examined the eye

before she left the hospital that Friday morning. He was a slim man with an artistic, sympathetic, but strong, face and gentle manner. He had been at work since eight o'clock, but managed to convey that she was the only patient in his world.

'You've done splendidly,' he said with a smile. 'Now go down to the country, take things easily . . . have a sherry in the evening and watch television in moderation . . . you've got the notes on what not to do.' He paused. 'Then come to see me in a fortnight.'

'Shall I be able to return to the flat, then?' She looked at him somewhat appealingly.

'We shall have to see how you progress; but, quite probably.'

'Thank you for all you've done.'

He smiled broadly to suggest that it was nothing.

There were, or had been, a dozen questions she had intended asking him, but she was incapable of remembering one. He was a busy man; he had other patients to see; operations lined up. Her questions could wait.

He left with a firm handshake, making her feel that she hadn't anything in the world to worry about.

It was strange, she thought, with the bandage off. The sight in her eye was as blurred as an out-of-focus photograph, while around the images and shapes, an almost startlingly clear picture of certain objects stood out at crazy angles. Lights threw off reflections like an illuminated tennis-racket without the handle, its strings creating filigree patterns in bright gold, suspended in space some feet away from the object. Everything bright also threw off prisms of dazzling light which hurt, and was relieved by the dark glasses given her to use. Walking gave her a strange sensation as though the floor was not quite in the right place and, at times, she might have been on an escalator. The word 'confidence' slid into her mind. Time would restore that. At the moment the world was a fantasy of distorting mirrors. It had been an interesting experience, but now the real adjustments had to be made. She felt relieved that Anita was collecting her, and that after calling at the flat, they would be alone on the journey to Sussex. Funny how she had grown accustomed to that hospital room; to the familiar routine, the cheerful faces of nurses; the frequent visits of friends and the general orderly 'chaos' of hospital life.

There was an atmosphere of expectancy as she waited for Anita; the hands of the clock appearing not to move. Her thoughts darted about without sequence. Anita wouldn't be late, and it was not yet eleven. Ross said he would call in at the flat . . . Glynis would come down to Monk's Corner at sometime during the weekend . . . A certain suspense seemed to hang in the air as she reflected on Ross, and Glynis, and their future. Her brows puckered as some nebulous worry, like a dark shadow, flashed across the screen of her mind, vanishing as she saw Anita come into the room. There followed the usual last-minute farewells.

'Thank you, Sister, for being so kind . . . thank you, Nurse.'

And then the moment when she faced daylight, outside, in the sun. The dazzling brightness, the over-exposed, curiously distorted scene, and the unbelievable greenness of the trees; the colours of the flowers around Buckingham Palace—the vastness.

'Nothing is real,' she said to Anita. 'Before, everything was muted and faintly hazy. Now, even the distortion seems magnified.'

'When you eventually get your spectacles, the definition will be marvellous,' Anita assured her. And while Anita was understanding and interested in Janet's reactions, her innermost thoughts concentrated on the fact that Ross would be at the Devonshire Street flat . . . provided nothing happened to prevent him, of course.

He arrived almost at the same moment as Anita (driving Janet's car) pulled up. And while his attentions were given to Janet, he flashed Anita an intent intimate look as though the memory of the previous evening lingered. Just then it was all she asked.

Janet said, when they were settled in the little morning room drinking their coffee, 'Glynis will be coming down with you tomorrow.' It was a statement of fact open to correction.

'No arrangements have been made,' Ross commented. 'Fleur wants Glynis to have dinner with her tomorrow evening, so I understand. But we'll certainly be with you for lunch on Sunday. If I can get away even late tomorrow, I shall do so. It's always best for me to travel alone.' He caught Anita's glance as he spoke, and allowed it to linger. 'Not that I don't prefer a passenger!'

'Depending on the passenger,' Anita said.

'How true.' His smile brought an atmosphere of harmony. He was like a man who had come to terms with himself, his problems solved. Yet what had changed, unless he now appreciated his own foolishness over Kenneth? A bubble of happiness touched her. She would be seeing him at the weekend; be in the same house with him. Life seemed full of promise.

Kenneth telephoned to inquire after Janet, and spoke to her. She was persuasive about the weekend and he promised to at least spend the day with them on Sunday.

When Janet put down the receiver she said quietly, 'Everyone has been so kind.'

'I'll put the drops in your eye before we leave,' Anita said suddenly. 'You must have them four times a day."

Janet took a sheet of paper from her handbag. 'Instructions,' she said with a smile.

Both Ross and Anita read it in turn.

DO NOT 1. Bend your head down, e.g. bending over a basin or picking up something from the floor, or gardening. Lift heavy weights.

  2. Screw up, knock, or rub your eye.

  3. Wash your own hair for at least two weeks. Hairdresser may wash hair, with head tilted backwards.

  4. Go back to work until the eye doctor has given you permission.

DO 1. Take life quietly; take care when going up and down stairs.

  2. Put in drops and ointments as required. No pad or bandage

necessary. Wear dark glasses if eyes are sensitive to light.

3. If necessary bathe eyes with salt solution, to be made up as follows:—1 pint of boiled water, mix in one teaspoonful of salt. Allow to cool before use.

N.B. You may read and write in moderation, also watch TV

The eye, when Janet took off her dark glasses, was blood-shot, a little swollen and bruised-looking, but medically entirely satisfactory. Janet didn't say that there was quite a bit of discomfort before the drops were due, and relief afterwards.

'And now I must go,' Ross said. 'I can leave you in good hands.' He added, 'Thank heaven.'

'Yes; bless Anita,' Janet murmured fervently. 'I must say I feel stupid and clumsy at the moment.' She laughed. 'Not quite "with it".'

'That's why you've got to take life quietly,' Ross reminded her. 'No matter what the operation, reaction sets in *after* you leave hospital. A quiet day tomorrow will be just what you need.' He stooped and kissed her cheek. 'Glad it's all over,' he said gently. 'I'll ring about seven tonight.' He added, 'Get to bed early.'

'I'll see to that,' Anita put in. Again, there was the thrill of intimacy in the parting look they exchanged and, as she glanced towards Janet, she noticed an expression almost of surprised enquiry on Janet's face which made her say swiftly, 'And now I'll pack up the car.'

As she went about her task she asked herself a

trifle anxiously if Janet suspected her attraction for Ross. The possibility disturbed her. A warning note sounded as she realised how dark glasses enabled the wearers to see every shade of expression on the faces of those around them, while concealing their own.

Glynis telephoned, chasing Ross and sorry she could not get in. 'We can't both be away from things,' she insisted to Janet, adding that she knew Janet understood about her dinner with Fleur the following evening.

'Of course I understand,' Janet exclaimed.

There was something a little ghostly, Anita thought, about arriving at Monk's Corner without Ross; its beauty seemed almost a mockery, and as she turned into the leafy winding lane that led to the drive, there came a tug at her heart and she said involuntarily, 'Seems very strange to be coming here without Ross.' The words rushed out, and she went on hurriedly, 'But it is a beautiful house, and you must love it . . . the *roses*, the colour—' She stopped. 'How does it look to you?'

'Technicolour, slightly distorted. I can see it all, but not as you understand sight, nor as I *have* known it.' She removed her spectacles and quickly replaced them. 'The light hurts—that's because I haven't any lens in my eye now, isn't it?' Janet laughed. 'I remember Sister telling me that. And Martin Jayson explained to me that although I have good sight in my left eye, the operated one is like a distorting mirror putting things out of focus.'

Jakes and his wife appeared at the doorway to greet them.

'A cup of tea,' Janet said after the greetings and

inquiries were over. The sunlight dappled the oak-panelled hall, glinting on the highly-polished wood-block floors. Flowers were massed in copper and brass; the smell of summer—of honeysuckle and briar-roses and all the subtly blended scents of the countryside—sweetened the breeze that wafted through the windows and open front door. Anita sighed with appreciation, helped Janet upstairs to her room, asking if she would like tea to be brought to her.

'Oh, no! We'll have it in the drawing-room! I want to see everything!'

Anita unpacked for her a little later, talked to Mrs Jakes so that there should be no lack of communication, and agreed that 'Mrs Wyndham looked very well'. A rapport was thus established! Nurses and staff were not always compatible, Anita knew. Jakes was 'the old school', nearing sixty, but with the energy and stamina of someone half his age.

Silence lay upon the land like a benediction. And as Anita sat back in the high Regency chair and sipped her tea, she thought of the weeks ahead without Ross; without the daily contact—to say nothing of the emotional upheaval and the uncertainty.

'I feel guilty about your having to be here like this,' Janet said, 'but it's lovely to have you here; you're so peaceful and you do everything so expertly and quietly . . . Oh, yes, you do. You would never have suited Ross at Harley Street had it been otherwise!' She was watching Anita carefully as she spoke, and waiting for her comment.

Anita lowered her gaze and tried to keep the

colour from rising to her cheeks, feeling slightly
nervous. Ross's name had significance, and she
knew she must behave with a natural casualness not
easy to achieve when he dominated her thoughts.

Suddenly, like thunder crashing into sunshine,
Janet said, 'I expect we shall have a wedding here
before very long . . . Not that the news will come as
any surprise to you.'

Anita felt that her lips had suddenly gone dry,
and she moistened them before echoing, 'Wedding', as though the word burned her.

Janet looked indulgent. 'Yes. Ross and Glynis.
Their marriage has always been a foregone conclusion. It's only a question of announcing the engagement. I thought you would have guessed.' Janet
had become uneasy about Anita's feelings for Ross
and fearful lest she might be hurt through ignor-
ance, or deliberate blindness.

Anita felt physically sick. She might have *wondered*, even have convinced herself that there was
some secret tie between Ross and Glynis, but it was
in moments of annoyance or anger.

'No,' she managed to say, 'not really. I accepted
the guardian and ward relationship—' She paused
because while the statement was true, it in no way
conveyed the conflicting emotions associated with
the assessment.

Janet's voice was gentle, 'Ross has been very
protective; not wanting to rush things. And now
that this operation of mine is over . . . well—' Janet
smiled. 'It's time now that Glynis married. She's
always doted on Ross, of course.'

Anita's thoughts were racing with her heart.
What a fool she had been! Ross had merely wanted

sexual excitement where she, herself, was concerned, taking advantage of his freedom, using it
until the last minute. And she had been weak
enough to allow emotion to rob her of all common
sense, accepting his relationship with Glynis,
blatantly deceiving herself for no better reason
than she *wanted* to be blind because his attraction
was so overpowering. She felt Janet's gaze upon
her, behind the dark glasses, and struggled to remain calm, to keep her voice steady as she said, 'I
suppose I've been too involved with my job to
notice the obvious. Guardians so often marry their
wards, anyway!' She gave a little empty laugh
which made Janet feel more than ever justified in
mentioning the subject, and thus sparing Anita the
ultimate shock. A sad little sensation touched
Janet's heart because she knew that her instinct had
been right, and that Anita was more than attracted
to Ross. A not difficult state of affairs to envisage,
since all women found him magnetic. A shadow fell
across the day. Janet did not pursue the subject.
She had only the satisfaction that now Anita was
forearmed, while hating the knowledge that she
had, also, been hurt. The evidence was in her eyes.

Ross, to their surprise, arrived unexpectedly for
lunch the following day, Saturday. Glynis was remaining with Fleur and Ross had revised his
appointments, giving him the extra hours.

Anita looked at him with a terrible sense of loss.
Now she *knew*. The question was how to extricate
herself from the untenable situation without betraying chagrin, jealousy or anger. His manner was
pleasant, but a little sombre, like that of a man with
something preying on his mind.

'I shall have a little rest this afternoon,' Janet said when lunch was over and they'd drunk their coffee.

'Then perhaps we could go for a walk,' Ross suggested, looking at Anita.

'That would be pleasant,' she said formally, but her heart quickened its beat, suspense increased, and she quickly averted her gaze from his.

They set off after she had settled Janet down, seeing that everything Janet required was to hand. It was a perfect day and Anita followed where Ross led as they climbed to a cradle in the panoramic downs and eventually sat down on grass that was soft and sweet beneath them, while the breeze held the sensuous fragrance of wild flowers, and a tang from the distant sea. Again that sharp sensual awareness alerted them, drugging her senses, obliterating anger, jealousy and pain, so that as his arms went around her and his lips found hers, she yielded in a spasm of longing as though she were clinging to hope itself. Then, almost fiercely, she drew back, outraged by the fact that, despite the circumstances, she was on the edge of making love, his power over her all-consuming.

And then suddenly, almost solemnly, he said 'I love you.'

She heard the words disbelievingly and they touched some raw spot in her heart, which stimulated an anger such as she had never know before in her life; an anger suffocating, terrifying in its intensity, as she cried, '*Love!* You don't know the meaning of the word; you're going to marry Glynis, and I don't want to hear anything you have to say. You're a philanderer, Ross; charming, deceitful, wanting the best of both worlds—even your patients are part of the romantic scene! Oh, no doubt you keep it within the bounds of morality; quiet little dinners . . . Fleur Sheriden—'

He stared at her, shocked, disbelieving, before he thundered, 'Have you quite finished?'

The tone of his voice withered her, awakening her to the madness and enormity of all she had said. Appalled by her own fury, tortured by the pain that twisted and turned in her body like some evil presence, robbing her of all control, leaving her at the mercy of what she knew then to be her love for him . . . the love she had hidden even from herself, and which now was a desperate seering agony, whipped up by a jealousy new and devastating. She had put the world between them, and nothing could repair the damage.

Ross had got to his feet. He was white, his expression grim and forbidding.

She wanted to cry out, but she was too choked to speak. And what could she say? He *was* going to marry Glynis. *I love you* . . . Wasn't that the philanderer speaking? The man desirous and intent upon making love? But neither argument, nor excuse, could alter the fact that the words she had uttered would haunt her for the rest of her life. The scenery around them, with its gold and blue and green, mocked her; the soft breeze cooling her cheeks seemed like an arctic wind cutting into her flesh.

Ross began to walk, to retrace the steps they had taken; she followed, stumbling now and then; once he reached out to prevent her falling, his touch electrifying her. She loved him. Fool not to have realised it before. The misery in her heart was like a weight, sickening, unendurable. No word was spoken; and he did not look at her when, reaching the drive, he turned and walked away to the side of the house, allowing her to go inside alone. She reached her room blindly, sitting on the edge of the bed, staring vacantly into space. What else would he have said, had she not begun her tirade? What would happen now? She could not leave Janet and, even if she felt like it, an apology would have seemed an insult.

'I expect we shall have a wedding here before long. It's only a question of announcing the engagement.'

Why couldn't he have been honest with her? Why pretend? Yet what *had* he pretended? she was forced to ask herself. And she knew with self-contempt that, if she were honest, it was still the fact that he was going to marry Glynis that was torturing her far more than the defect in his character. Her love for him was like a fever engulfing her. Why had she realised it only when she knew she had lost him?

A silence, almost of death, lay upon the house. She dragged herself to the window and saw his tall figure walking towards his car. Without looking around, he got into it and raced down the drive—the gesture seemed eloquent of a prison door closing on her, shutting her out of the world. At that moment her control vanished and she buried her face in her hands as great sobs tore at her.

Later, she heard Janet moving about, and met her on the landing to pilot her down the stairs.

'Did you have a good walk?' Janet immediately noticed how pale and strained Anita looked.

'Yes, thank you. Ross went out in the car afterwards.'

'Probably gone over to see Philip and Fay . . . but he usually says,' Janet murmured half to herself, feeling apprehensive.

Ross returned for tea. And if he had deliberately devised an exquisite form of torture, he could not have chosen one more calculated to wound than his meticulous correctness and the dexterity with which he selected subjects of conversation in which Anita had no part, but which Janet was able to enjoy.

And when they had almost finished tea, Glynis telephoned. Ross took the call.

'Something wrong?'

Anita could not take her gaze from his face.

'I'm at Uckfield! The car broke down . . . Carburettor.'

'Don't sound so aggressive.' He laughed as he spoke. 'Of course, I'll come and get you. Only about fourteen miles, and Janet may like the run.' He looked across at Janet who said immediately that she would. 'Ah, well, we'll sort the return journey out. Kenneth will be down tomorrow . . . Like Grand Central Station. Have a cup of tea somewhere. Yes; I know the garage, or at least, *where* it is.'

He replaced the receiver; reiterated a little of what had been said, adding, 'The garage people can't do the repair until Monday.'

'Everything stops on Saturday and Sunday,' Janet observed. 'Will you come with us, Anita?'

Ross was standing looking out over the grounds. He did not turn.

'No thank you,' Anita said, struggling to infuse a note of lightness into her voice. 'I'll be lazy and read.' She added swiftly, 'I'll get your handbag . . . you don't need a coat. Scarf?'

'Handbag and scarf . . . Stairs make me feel that I'm toppling over . . . funny sensation.'

Anita fetched the handbag and scarf, and walked with Janet to the car, seeing her into it.

Ross joined them and slid into the driving seat. 'All right?' he said to Janet.

'Perfectly.'

He neither looked at, nor spoke to Anita, who, as she went back into the house, felt ill. This was not, she reasoned, a lovers' quarrel, or anything she had ever experienced before. Yet was it anything for which she could apologise and retain any dignity? Wasn't it a case of too much having been said already? Terrifying what a matter of minutes, even seconds, could do; seconds, and a few words. The hands of the clock could never be put back. And did she want them to be, seeing that Ross could be such a philanderer? Conflict gnawed at her. He had not made any promises. He had made love to her, and she had allowed him to do so believing him to be free, no matter how suspicion had sometimes crept into the situation. She went up to her room again as though it offered the only sanctuary possible. The thought of Kenneth obtruded. He would be with them tomorrow. *Kenneth* . . . she had no doubt about his love for her, or his loyalty. Ross, what did he know of love? She tried to whip up anger again, to denigrate him so that the hurt might lessen. But it didn't. She dreaded the evening ahead, seeing him with

Glynis, knowing they were to be married. In that moment she felt an outsider, excommunicated.

Glynis was not in the best of moods on her arrival, and when she saw Anita she said bluntly, '*You* look washed out . . . Been a maddening kind of day. I detest cars when they don't go. Infuriates me.' She sighed. 'Thank heaven for Ross . . .' She called out to him.

He walked into the hall where she and Anita were standing. 'What's wrong?'

'Nothing now . . . but how about taking me to the Hungry Monk at Jevington tonight? Janet won't want to go and Anita's here to keep her company . . . we've a lot to catch up on. Don't seem to have had any time really to ourselves lately.'

Ross said immediately, 'If that's what you'd like, by all means. Janet will understand.'

'Janet would hate it if we stayed in,' Glynis observed.

Janet overheard that as she crossed the hall.

'I certainly would,' she agreed.

'If you really *did* feel like coming,' Glynis suggested hesitantly.

'I don't,' Janet retorted with a smile, 'and I'd be about as welcome as a snow storm!'

Anita stood there, paralysed by her own unhappiness. She looked at Ross but she might not have been there as he said, 'I'll see if I can get a table. It will be a miracle. They're always heavily booked.'

'You'll manage it . . . just turn on your charm!'

Anita heard the word 'charm' and, with it, the

echo of her words, '*You're a philanderer, charming, deceitful—*'

No flicker of recollection crossed Ross's face; he moved in the direction of his study to make the telephone call. And at that moment, Glynis uttered a smothered cry, 'I think I'm going to faint—'

He swung round just in time to see Anita catch the swaying figure.

Purposefully Ross substituted Anita's arms for his own, and carried Glynis into the drawing room so that she could lie on the sofa. Anita swiftly got a towel from the cloakroom, wrung it out in cold water, returned, and handed it to him so that he could place it behind Glynis's neck.

Glynis stirred. 'What happened . . .'

'You fainted,' he said, his tone anxious.

Anita fetched a glass of water. Ross supported Glynis's shoulders as she sipped it.

Janet, who had remained silent and calm in the background, said, 'We're certainly in good hands.'

Glynis sat up, sighed, and exclaimed rather testily, 'Don't fuss . . . you've seen a woman faint before, Ross.'

'But not you,' he said gently.

The words pierced Anita's heart like a knife. How convincing he was; his voice modulated to just the right note, as it was when he had said, 'I love you', only that short while before.

'I don't think I want to go to Jevington.' Glynis spoke abruptly. 'A quiet evening.'

'Doctor's orders,' Ross insisted, putting a hand over hers. 'Just rest for a bit.'

She gave a little sigh and looked up at him with an

intimate smile. 'You're so good to me,' she murmured.

'That isn't difficult,' he said quietly.

It was amazing, Anita thought later, how an entire evening could pass, a meal be eaten, without Ross addressing one single remark to her. Glynis, only partially recovered from her faint, took full advantage of the consideration and attention shown to her.

Ross and Anita were alone for only a very short while immediately before bed-time.

'I'd be grateful,' he said without betraying feeling of any kind, 'if you would remain until after Janet has seen Martin Jayson. It would distress her if you were to leave now. After that I shall not trouble you further. Nurse Pettifer will be happy to stay on until my plans are finalised.'

Anita stood as though life itself was draining away from her. This cold dismissal was a little death, and she said, the words torn from her, 'Ross, I—'

'Spare me any hypocrisy,' he rapped out icily. 'You made your opinion abundantly clear. Suppose we leave it at that.'

Before she could speak again he turned and strode from the room.

CHAPTER NINE

ANITA hardly knew how she lived through Sunday. Gloom lay upon the house like a pall so far as she was concerned, and the effort of keeping up, and being cheerful, was almost more than she could endure. Kenneth's gaze was puzzled and suspicious, and he disbelieved her when she insisted that she was perfectly all right.

'If you ask me,' he said testily, 'no one is all right. It's like a charade.'

She flashed at him, 'You're not exactly the life and soul of the party.'

'Depression is catching,' he retorted. 'Have you had a row with Ross?' There was jealousy in his voice.

'Ross?' she exclaimed uneasily. 'Why should I?'

'I asked the question; don't answer it by asking another . . . I don't like your being stuck down here, anyway,' he mumbled.

Janet said, when eventually Ross, Glynis and Kenneth had left that Sunday evening, 'It hasn't been a happy weekend. There's *something*.'

Anita didn't attempt to contradict her. Janet was far too observant to be deceived.

The following week passed in a haze of unhappiness, each day and hour dragging interminably while bringing Anita's ultimate departure perilously close. The weather was perfect, and while Janet was a friendly companion, Anita ached to be at

Harley Street, the schism between herself and Ross an increasing agony. Why had she lost control? What she had said was undoubtedly true, but if only she had not said it so stormily.

Ross and Glynis telephoned every day until, on Thursday, Janet said brightly, 'Ah, well! Ross and Glynis are coming down together tomorrow evening.'

Anita longed for, yet dreaded, the moment of Ross's arrival.

He greeted her with a polite, yet blank, acknowledgement, talking of Janet as if to establish merely Anita's professional association. Glynis meanwhile seemed to follow his every movement, taking note of each word he uttered, hardly letting him out of her sight.

'You'll be missing Kenneth,' she said suddenly to Anita at lunch-time on Saturday. 'Pity he has to work this weekend.'

Ross exclaimed, his voice cutting, 'You could have gone back to your flat while Glynis and I are here . . . it didn't occur to me until now; although, with Kenneth working, he wouldn't have much time to spare.'

Glynis, bored with the conversation, turned to Ross, 'Let's go for a walk this afternoon. I need some fresh air, and I'm sick of driving, or being driven. The traffic gets worse,' she added petulantly, 'so noisy and smelly. I wouldn't care if I never saw London again.' She looked at Ross rather anxiously. 'Would you mind leaving London—if it were possible?'

There was a second of tense silence before Ross replied, 'As I like the best of both worlds, I enjoy

London as well as the country.' With that he looked straight into Anita's eyes and then turned away.

Anita paled; she felt hot and cold and faintly sick. The words lashed her like a whip.

When the meal was over, Anita saw Janet to her room.

'What are you going to do?' Janet asked solicitously. 'I'm afraid you're having a very dull time, my dear.'

Anita forced a smile. 'Not at all; it's good to be lazy . . . Nothing else you need?'

Janet gave a little sigh. 'I might have a little sleep, but I get tired of having to lie on one side. My eye feels rough and sore today. Is that the healing business?'

Anita assured her that it was.

'Not being able to bend down,' Janet murmured, 'gets tiresome. Have you ever tried to brush your teeth and rinse your mouth out, standing upright?' She laughed. 'Also people don't realise how much they nod and shake their head, until they're told not to do it! I could watch television, but the picture is very dazzling and distorted as if the wind is blowing it all to the right. And I see double sometimes! Sounds crazy, doesn't it?' She added, 'But apparently it is normal with cataracts! They're temperamental things if you ask me!'

'Won't be long before you see Mr Jayson—Wednesday next.' Anita felt a pang. She had not mentioned the fact that she would be leaving Harley Street. And dreaded having to do so.

Meanwhile, downstairs, sitting on the patio, Glynis said to Ross, 'I feel sorry for Anita today.'

'Why?' Ross was immediately alert.

'Because she seems lost without Kenneth . . . They're lovers, of course,' she added with pleasant casualness. 'Kenneth is mad about her.'

'You exaggerate,' Ross said.

'Because I'm talking of Anita?' She paused and looked at him with directness. 'You're pretty off-hand with her these days. Or don't you realise?'

'I realise,' he said firmly, 'that I've no desire to discuss any of this. What Anita does with her life is her own business.'

'I was not *criticising* her,' Glynis protested, wide-eyed, 'and I'm not making anything up. Kenneth told me that he wanted to marry her.' Glynis laughed. 'You must have realised?'

Ross retorted, 'I do not concern myself with—' he stopped, then, 'Oh, for goodness' sake let's go for that walk, and stop this gossip.'

'No need to be beastly,' Glynis protested.

'I'm sorry.'

She shot him an apprehensive glance, and moved to his side as they got up from their respective chairs, slipping her arm through his. An expression of fierce determination hardened her face.

That evening Glynis urged Ross to take her, and Janet, to the Hungry Monk at Jevington, since they had been deprived of the visit the previous week. Anita had made it plain that there was a play on television she would like to watch. Janet had tried to persuade her to join them and then stopped abruptly when she sensed the anxiety Anita was striving to conceal.

It was a lonely evening as Anita settled down to watch the David Storey play, losing concentration, despite its compelling qualities. Her life was chaotic in every respect, she realised, and the prospect of finding another job filled her with trepidation. Ambition, enthusiasm, were dead. She refused dinner and asked Jakes for coffee which he brought with some anxiety, as he and his wife decided that Nurse Fielding was 'not herself'.

It was with relief, however, that Anita finally heard Ross's car returning, its wheels braking on the gravel immediately outside the front door.

'We had a lovely meal,' Janet said in greeting, 'but I wish you'd been there.' How pale, she thought, Anita looked.

Glynis turned to Janet somewhat perfunctorily, 'You must be tired.' She was annoyed that Janet had accepted the invitation, particularly since she had tactfully declined it the previous week. Janet had actually gone on impulse, feeling instinctively that Ross had wished for her company.

Anita concentrated on Janet, said goodnight to Ross and Glynis, and saw Janet to bed, returning downstairs to collect a newspaper for herself.

Voices came from the study, the door of which was partly open.

Anita stood transfixed as she heard Glynis say confidently, 'Let's not waste any more time, darling. Let's get married now.'

Ross's reply was swift and firm, 'The sooner the better.'

As Anita managed to tiptoe past the open door, she saw Glynis in his arms.

Now there was nothing more to be said, she thought dully, just as there was no possible room for doubt.

The following morning Anita got up early and went, almost defiantly, for a swim in the pool. How different it all was from the first time she swam there. Then, her world had been full of excitement and promise, high-lighted by the lingering ecstasy of Ross's first kiss. Now, it held nothing but the heartache that was like a physical weight lying heavily upon her. As she struck out through the clear sparkling water, emotion whipped up resolve. No matter what she, herself, had contributed to the final break with Ross, the fact remained that Glynis had always been in the picture, and now always would be. Colour rose in her cheeks with embarrassment; Kenneth had known this, but had obviously respected that knowledge as sacrosanct. Looking back on it all, she realised how Kenneth had lightened the burden of her own conflict, and she wished he could be with her now. Idly she turned over and floated, just at the moment Ross appeared through the main entrance.

'Good morning,' he called out formally.

'Good morning.' She moved smoothly into an upright position, arms hardly rippling the water. She felt that he must hear her heart thudding.

He plunged in, swimming strongly until he reached her side. The coldness had gone from his eyes as he said in business-like tones, 'I'm glad to have this opportunity of talking . . . I don't know what plans you have in mind so far as Janet is concerned next week after you have seen Martin Jayson, but I wouldn't like her to be upset by your going.' He paused before adding, 'Whatever the circumstances, I appreciate your care of her.'

The storm had died between them; there was no

more room for anger. His future was secure, Anita argued, and he could afford the luxury of indifference where she, herself, was concerned.

'Helping Janet has been a pleasure.' Anita's voice was very quiet. 'You have not told her about my leaving Harley Street?'

'No; as I said, I don't want her upset. Once she is back at the flat, and able to move about more freely, it will be different.'

Anita took the initiative, drawing on courage, her manner calm and professional. 'May I suggest, then, that *I* tell her I've decided to change my job? It would be simple, seeing that you have Nurse Pettifer.'

There came a sudden awareness of each other as though the ghosts of yesterday danced between them on the cool water.

'That,' he said jerkily, 'would be an excellent idea.'

'Then I'll wait until after I've been with her to see Mr Jayson.' For a second she dared to meet his gaze, 'I take it that you have no objection to my working in the Harley Street area?' Faint cynicism crept into her voice.

He averted his gaze for a second and then, his expression wholly inscrutable, replied, 'I have no jurisdiction over anything you do, Anita.' Stillness lay upon them before he added, 'You are a free agent.'

Anita winced at the finality.

A voice reached them across the pool, 'So *here* you are. Why didn't you call me, Ross?'

Anita thought bitterly that it was like a replay of the first time she'd visited the pool and Glynis had appeared, faintly disgruntled.

Now she plunged into the water and joined them, looking questioningly from face to face, then addressing Anita, exclaimed, 'Has Ross told you?'

'Told me what?' Anita managed to say coolly.

'That he and I are going to be married.' She hastened with a little, rather high-pitched laugh, 'Not that the news will come as a surprise to anyone.'

An awkward breathless silence fell. Ross darted a glance at Anita whose expression was faintly mocking and ironical as she said, 'No, it hasn't come as a surprise, I assure you.' She added her good wishes.

Glynis rushed on, 'We shall probably slip away somewhere quietly; neither of us wants a musical comedy wedding.' She smiled up at Ross. 'Do we darling?'

Ross didn't hesitate, 'True.' The agreement was expressionless.

Anita was aware of Ross's nearness, of his strong lean body within such a short distance of her own. What was he thinking? Even *remembering*?

He said abruptly, striking out as he spoke, 'I'll leave you two to—' The rest of the sentence was lost as he darted away and disappeared from the pool.

Glynis' gaze followed him. She looked smugly self-satisfied. Suddenly she cried out, 'Oh . . . I feel funny . . . *Anita*—'

Anita immediately supported her, propelling her weakening body to the tiled surround, managing almost to tip her on to it and into a sitting position, holding her head down to prevent a faint.

'So *stupid*,' Glynis cried, annoyed, even petulant. 'It isn't the heat this *morning*.' She looked white and shaken.

A shudder went over Anita; a sensation that seemed to lift the skin from her flesh, as the realisation swept over her: *Glynis was pregnant*.

Anita's reaction, her expression of alarmed astonishment, communicated itself to Glynis who cried irritably, 'Don't look at me like that! I'm perfectly all right,' she added foolishly, 'and I don't want any fuss; or for you to mention it.' She shot Anita a warning glance. 'I hate discussions about health. And I've enough doctors around me, heaven knows.'

'All the more reason why you should avail yourself of their services when you need them,' Anita suggested, the sick sensation of disillusionment increasing as she thought of Ross. It didn't matter how great the suspicion had been, proof was a death knell.

Glynis breathed deeply, stretched herself, and said a trifle defiantly, 'I have Ross to look after me. We both need a break. Oh, I know I had that winter holiday, but I didn't *enjoy* being away from him.' She got to her feet. 'Now that Janet is all right, we can go off on our honeymoon at any time. We'd thought of Madeira . . .'

'*The sooner the better*'. How significant Ross's words were in the circumstances.

Anita made no comment and Glynis rushed on, 'By the way, I understand that, after today, I shan't be seeing you again. Ross told me you weren't returning to Harley Street, but that Janet didn't know yet. Thank heaven Nurse Pettifer is so reliable, and will be able to hold the fort while we're away. Ross's friend and colleague, in Wimpole Street, will deputise so Ross won't have any worries . . . Is it your intention to return to hospital life?'

Anita felt churned up and indignant, although she realised it was perfectly reasonable for Ross to have discussed the situation with Glynis. Standing there, knowing precisely what his relationship with Glynis was, and had been, she shuddered at her own vulnerability and his betrayal of them both.

'No,' she replied firmly. 'I shall stay in the Harley Street area. My flat is there.'

Glynis softened; a wistful, almost apologetic, look came into her eyes. 'Of course; how silly of me . . . and thank you for being so good to Janet.'

Anita forced a smile. It was like walking down a long dark tunnel without any light at the end.

Janet received the news of the engagement with indulgent acceptance. There was no element of surprise. Almost to Anita's relief, Philip and Fay Adams called that morning for drinks, Glynis having telephoned to invite them. Ross met Anita's gaze for a fraction of a second as Fay entered the room, and there was no doubting the power of the memory that flashed between them; or the withering scorn in her eyes which, she knew, shocked him. The comparative calm of the moments at the pool was completely eradicated. His voice lost a little of its depth, as he greeted Fay, and his smooth air of authority deserted him. Anita was human enough to feel a thrill of triumph because, at least, she had the ability to make him uncomfortable.

'It's good to see you again,' Fay said to her. 'A

happy day today,' she added warmly, flashing a smile in Ross and Glynis' direction.

A terrible homesickness surged over Anita as she listened to the conversation that followed. She longed to be back in her own flat where she could privately fight her emotional battle without having to put on an act. She found herself aching with gentle envy as she looked at Philip and Fay Adams: they were so obviously happy together, their harmony like the echo of music. And even as she despised Ross so, ironically, she loved him the more.

It was Janet who said, 'This calls for champagne, Ross.' There was a note of surprise in her voice because he had not asked Jakes to serve it.

Corks popped a little later, a toast was drunk, and Anita noticed that Glynis had only a sip from her glass, almost as though she had taken a dislike to it, where previously it had been a favourite. Anita studied her, half-fascinated; half-repelled. Ross's child . . . Glynis had lain in his arms; known the passion of his kiss, the fierce possessiveness of his arms. Inwardly Anita groaned, so intense was the pain of memory.

When evening came Ross sought her out as she sat in the garden alone—deliberately absenting herself.

'It will be unlikely that I shall see you again,' he said, his expression inscrutable. 'As I said this morning, thank you for all you've done.'

'I shall keep in touch with Janet,' she exclaimed with defiant firmness. 'Glynis told me that *she* knows I'm leaving.' There was an imperceptible pause before she added, 'And don't worry, I shall not come to your wedding in the event of Janet inviting me.' Her voice was without sarcasm.

'No one,' he said sternly, 'will come to my wedding. We shall slip away quietly somewhere and escape any fuss.'

Anita looked up at him from the cushioned hammock.

'Very wise,' she commented, staring him out. The thought struck her disturbingly: Was it possible that he did not yet *know* about the child?

'Goodbye, Anita,' he said solemnly, and moved quickly away.

Anita sat there until she heard the car going down the drive.

Anita drove Janet back to Janet's flat the following Wednesday. Everything was allowed for should Martin Jayson not give Janet the all-clear to return to a near-normal routine, and the cases left in the car in the event of their having to go back to Sussex.

But there was no problem; he was pleased with her; she could take up her life again, the restrictions over. In a short while she would have spectacles and since she had one good eye, her problems would then be over, apart from getting acclimatised to the lens.

It was not until later that day, when they had returned from Harley House and were sitting in the lofty high-ceilinged drawing room, having tea, that Anita told Jane she was leaving Ross.

Janet didn't start in either alarm or surprise. But she said quietly, 'I'm terribly sorry; but I must admit that I haven't "seen" your going back.'

Anita lowered her gaze and then raised it in an

honest steady look. 'Ross and I are no longer compatible.'

'That was evident,' Janet said gently. 'We can't always explain these things.' Janet knew then, what she had long suspected, that Anita was in love with him.

Anita urged, 'I'd like to feel that it won't make any difference to—to our—'

'Good heavens, no!' Janet interrupted. 'I'd hate us to lose touch. Perhaps, sometimes, when I go to Monk's Corner on my own, you might like to come there. Of course, I don't know what will happen after Ross and Glynis are married.'

There was a little understanding silence.

'And if ever you should need me for anything— anything at all—you've only to give me a ring,' Anita insisted.

Janet nodded. 'I'd certainly do that,' she said, and meant it.

When they parted Janet kissed her warmly. 'Just thank you,' she murmured, her eyes suspiciously bright.

Anita's key went into the lock of the front door of her flat a matter of minutes later. It welcomed her rather like a hot water bottle on a cold night. She could relax; not have to think, or plan and, for a little while at least, be free of all responsibility.

The telephone rang and she jumped as of old.

Kenneth said, 'Welcome home. Have I judged it about right?'

'To within five minutes.' Her spirits rose.

'Any brandy left from Christmas?' He laughed. 'Actually, if there isn't, I have a bottle which I'd like to bring over.'

Anita hesitated for a second, then asked herself, Why not? She hadn't Ross to think about now; no guilt, no complications.

'Do; give me time to have a shower and get out of my travelling clothes.'

'Splendid; I can't make it for an hour or so, anyway . . . Glad to be back?'

'Yes,' she said. 'Yes; I am.'

'I've just spoken to Janet. I hear she has the all-clear . . . She told me about Ross and Glynis. No surprise, of course.'

Anita tried to keep her voice steady.

'True; no surprise.' She hurried on, 'See you later, then.'

As she replaced the receiver she told herself that this was where she disciplined her thoughts and channelled them into a new dimension. She had to face the fact that Ross would soon be Glynis's husband, and that unless by co-incidence, she, herself, was unlikely ever to see him again. Once she had told Kenneth about leaving Harley Street, the chapter could be closed. A little wave of affection for Kenneth stole over her. His presence that evening would be exactly what she needed. Resolutely she got up from the chair, unpacked, showered, and was ready for him when he arrived. A shadow momentarily touched her: she had to remember that Kenneth loved her, and that she must not impose on his friendship, nor use him as a palliative.

'It's good to have you away from Monk's Corner,' he said in greeting, and looked around the sitting room with approval.

She said directly, meeting his gaze, 'I'm not

returning to Harley Street. Ross and I have reached the parting of the ways. I shall keep in touch with Janet, but that is all.'

Kenneth's expression reflected his relief, but not amazement.

'You can't expect me to shed any tears over that! I'm damned glad. I'm not going to ask you what went wrong. It doesn't matter.'

'You're a very understanding person,' she said.

He brushed the compliment aside. All he conceded was, 'You weren't happy, Anita. That's enough for me.' He put the brandy bottle down on the drinks tray, opened it, poured out two generous measures, raised his glass and said, 'To us?'

Their glasses met, held, and fell away.

'Just one thing,' he hastened, 'you'll appreciate that my friendship with Ross and Glynis—'

Anita cut in, 'Good gracious, *my* getting out of the picture, won't in any way affect *you*. There's no vendetta!'

He sighed and relaxed. 'Once they're married,' he commented, 'the pattern is bound to change, anyway.'

She nodded, and looked through into the bedroom where she and Ross had made love. His ghost seemed to linger there hauntingly, defying her to exorcise it. Would she ever be free of his presence? Or the hungry need, both mental and physical? If only, she thought, she were the type to seek solace in Kenneth's arms. Yet might not time enable her to accept the love he offered?

'Would you like to leave London?' he asked suddenly. 'Oh, I know you have the flat, but you could always let it.' He looked at her intently. 'I don't really mind where I go. It isn't where you *are* that matters, but with whom. I'd adapt, Anita; and I rather like the idea of a country practice . . . how would you fancy being *my* nurse?'

'I just fancy being a friend at the moment,' she told him. 'By the way, you don't happen to know anyone who's wanting a nurse—do you?'

'In the same capacity that you worked for Ross?'

'Yes.'

Kenneth surprised her by saying, 'As a matter of fact, I do. A Dr Wren. Charles Wren. He's a physician in Wimpole Street. Known him for years; we were students together. But *he* had ambition and a goal. His nurse is getting married, and he was bemoaning her loss only the other day. If you like, I'll speak to him tomorrow.'

'Would you?' Anita brightened. 'I want to get back to work again as soon as possible.'

'Well, you'll like Charles. Married; thirty-six; two children of eight and ten, and a very attractive wife. Settled without being dull. I envy him.'

'Sounds ideal.'

Kenneth gave her a significant look. 'Yes; bachelors can be temperamental!'

'You should know!' They laughed together and lapsed into silence.

'How about coming out with me on Sunday? And do you realise that you haven't yet seen *my* flat? True enough, I share it with a colleague and it's rather like Grand Central Station on occasion. Usually orderly chaos, but we'll tidy it up for you sometime . . . We could go on the river on Sunday. How about the Compleat Angler at Marlow?' He leaned forward in his chair. 'Say yes, Anita.'

'Yes,' she agreed without protest.

When it was time for him to leave, he leaned forward and kissed her lightly on the lips.

'Until Sunday,' he said, drawing back. 'I'll pick you up at about eleven-thirty. It's only just over thirty miles.'

Anita was hearing every word he said, but the sound seemed to come from a distance, as though she had ceased to be part of the scene. Being with Kenneth was both natural and, at the same time, foreign, because at that moment he had suddenly taken on an entirely different role, their destinies linked, the future almost pre-determined. The thought rushed through her mind that, with Kenneth, she would be able to hear all about Ross. That, also, she argued, would be true where Janet was concerned. Kenneth, however, was different. Did he suspect what her relationship with Ross had been? In any case, he was not the type of man who would expect to have all the sexual details of her life filled in. She went out to his car with him. The cobbled mews, flanked by quaint Georgian cottages, was bright with window-boxes boasting a variety of flowers, and the soft light of evening touched it with a certain old-fashioned magic, conjuring up fanciful pictures of carriages, instead of cars.

'I'll speak to Charles before he goes to his rooms,' Kenneth said as he got into the driving seat. 'He'll want you to start immediately.'

'Couldn't be better.'

'Strange,' Kenneth mused, giving her a quizzical look, 'when he spoke of losing his nurse, I told him that I knew of the ideal person, but she was in a job!

Just goes to show how little we know about tomorrow, and that nothing is impossible . . . not even your coming to Marlow with me on Sunday,' he added as he moved away.

Anita stood looking at the night sky now golden with reflected light. The traffic throbbed as a background noise rather than as an assault, and after the silence of Monk's Corner it seemed like the pulse of life. She went into the flat and shut the door with an air of finality. A chapter in her life was over.

During the next fortnight, Anita began working for Dr Wren, liking him immediately as a thoroughly pleasant family man, with a sense of humour and a considerate awareness of what her work entailed. He was almost as grateful to have found her as she to have found him, and they each blessed Kenneth for the introduction. At least, she thought, the grapevine would soon buzz in medical circles that 'Mr Wyndham's nurse had left and gone to Dr Wren' and, no doubt, the news would reach Ross's ears. She rightly sensed that Janet would not discuss her affairs. She had visited Janet once during her lunch hour, only to learn that Ross and Glynis were to be married quietly—within the next week or so—at a Register Office in Eastbourne. It struck her that Janet was not entirely composed as she talked of the plans which included a honeymoon at an hotel in the New Forest owned by relatives of a patient of Ross's, and to which they would drive immediately after the ceremony. It was to be purely a private affair without announcements or celebrations of any kind—at Glynis's request—and to which Ross was apparently thankful to agree.

Anita had listened, almost embarrassed by her own knowledge, and the fact that the wedding arrangements and general secrecy bore out the conviction.

Anita found that sleep eluded her during that vital period. She dragged herself from bed one Saturday morning at the end of July, with the thought racing through her mind: Was the wedding today? The carriage clock ticked noiselessly, and she seemed to be holding her breath as she watched, almost mesmerised, while its hands moved imperceptibly to six a.m.

The shrill ringing of the telephone set her nerves jangling. Who would be calling her at this hour?

But Janet's voice, panic-stricken, cried, 'Oh, Anita; please come . . . I can't wake Glynis! I think she's taken something by mistake . . . Russ is operating—some emergency. I don't even know the hospital.'

'I'll be with you in minutes,' Anita promised. Her voice rose, 'Try to rouse her. *Try*.'

CHAPTER TEN

ANITA reached Janet's flat and found that Glynis was in a state of semi-consciousness, almost pulseless. She lay like a rag doll, every now and then mumbling incoherently as though drunk.

'Ambulance, hospital,' Anita said immediately, going to the telephone and making the necessary calls.

'I can't believe it,' Janet murmured in distress. She indicated the half-empty bottle of Mogadon tablets.

'At least we know what drug we're dealing with,' Anita said with some relief as she lightly smacked and cajoled, raising her voice, trying to prevent Glynis slipping into unconsciousness. And all the time the question hammering in her brain was: Why?

'They were to have been married on Tuesday,' Janet said, devastated. 'I shouldn't have *known* she was like this, but I had to get up to go to the bathroom, and noticed her door was ajar. What made me look in? . . . Well, I can't imagine, but when I saw her sprawled out on the bed . . . Oh, *Anita!*'

Glynis was incapable of being roused sufficiently to stand up, or be given black coffee to counteract the overdose. But Anita kept talking to her, shaking her, knowing that every second was vital.

'Ross—' The name was called with slurred faintness.

The ambulance team arrived and Anita said, 'I'll go with her.' She looked at Janet, 'You get in touch with Ross the moment you can. I'll stay at the hospital until he arrives.'

Janet, white, stunned, cried, 'I don't know what I should have done without you . . . she *will* be all right?'

'They'll take her into intensive care,' Anita said reassuringly, relaxing for a second as she relinquished her charge. The silence and emptiness of the streets seemed a fitting accompaniment for the little procession as the stretcher slid into place and the ambulance doors closed on the world, while the team set to work, giving Glynis oxygen and an injection of piridoxine to counteract the effect of the drug in her blood. Anita sat there as if watching a fantasy film that linked up with her previous hospital life. The red of the blankets against the white paint-work; the antiseptic smell highlighting the drama. It was inconceivable that Glynis should wish to take her life a day or two before her marriage. Suspense, conjecture, fear, crept into the atmosphere.

Once they reached St Mark's, Anita was able to expedite matters by listing all the particulars, and Glynis was wheeled into intensive care, where she was examined, given a gastric lavage—or stomach wash-out—and put on a cardiac monitor with closed circuit television.

Anita had spoken to Janet and was allowed to see Glynis some time later. She was whoosy, partially aware of her surroundings, and looking frail and pathetic as she lay there in her white hospital garb, her eyes sunken in a mask-like face.

'I don't . . . want to be . . . here,' she murmured in a disjointed fashion. 'Ross—' She gave a little groan as though memory had rushed back and, with it, the pain and anguish which must have precipitated the crisis. With that she closed her eyes and drifted away again, clinging to Anita's hand like a child seeking comfort. Then, 'Don't leave me,' she cried. Her voice broke. 'Why . . . bring . . . me *back*?' Her gaze wandered around at the incredible mass of equipment, her brows puckered, her expression confused. 'And why have I . . . got this tube?' she complained, indicating the intravenous glucose drip. 'Don't want . . . I forget.' Then, gathering strength, she cried, 'You *know* . . . *they* mustn't. Anita; oh Anita, *help* me,' she pleaded. 'I'm . . . frightened—*frightened*.' Her eyes rounded and she gave a little cry.

Anita soothed her. 'No one will know,' she promised, guessing that Glynis was only a matter of weeks pregnant.

'And you won't—'

'I don't betray secrets,' Anita assured her.

'I don't . . . want to remember. I don't *want* to—' her voice rose.

A watching nurse stepped in view and took her pulse and blood pressure. She looked at Anita with understanding. When the patient could safely sleep naturally, the chances were that the drama would be over.

And as Anita sat there she was sub-consciously waiting for Ross to appear.

'*We are unlikely to see each other again* . . .'

How empty and futile all the anger and bitterness seemed in the face of near-death. Its dark shadow reduced everything to the simplicity of truth which mocked antagonism, and made feuds petty and futile.

At that moment he came into the unit, Sister at his side. His gaze went to the figure in the bed, and then to Anita who got up, about to leave. Glynis stirred instantly, 'Don't go . . . you *promised* . . .'

Ross flashed Anita a glance. 'Stay,' he said, drawing up a chair for himself.

Glynis turned her face away, like a contrite child who knows it has been naughty. Pathetically, she had become a child, as awareness ebbed and flowed leaving her vulnerable, and at the mercy of torturing memories which no one else could share.

Both Ross and Anita knew that in her present bemused state, while appearing not to register what was being said, every word reached her subconscious.

'Thank you,' Ross said to Anita. 'And thank God you were able to take over.'

Pity stirred as she looked at him. He was grave, bewildered, and avoided her direct gaze. The situation, she argued, could only place him at a painful disadvantage, and Anita had no desire to add to his distress. It was strange how in those moments, keeping vigil at Glynis's bedside, she discovered the real meaning of the word, love; and knew that embodied in it was compassion, sympathy; a desire to spare hurt, not to cause it. She wanted to comfort him, no matter what unhappiness he might have caused her; and longed to put out a hand and touch his with a gentleness that might assuage, in some measure, a little of his grief. But all she said was, 'She will recover—only that matters.'

He nodded, and spoke in a whisper, 'I can't believe it; she seemed perfectly all *right*, full of plans, when we parted last night.'

'Time answers all our questions.'

'Does it, Anita?' His voice was deep and low; his expression that of a tortured man. 'I wish I could believe that.'

Glynis stirred, whispered Ross's name and cried, 'I'm so . . . *sorry*.' She sighed wearily. 'So tired.' With that she closed her eyes and dozed.

Sister said encouragingly, 'Everything seems stable. Why don't you go and get some coffee?'

Ross glanced at the cardiac monitor, satisfied by what he saw.

'Thank you, Sister. We'll do as you suggest.'

Coffee. With Ross. Anita's pulse quickened. She slipped her hand from Glynis' grasp.

Glynis was allowed home two days later. Normally she would have had to see a psychiatrist, but since she was in Ross's care, the routine was dispensed with. Ross had only once questioned her during that time, and she said imploringly, 'Don't ask me . . . Later . . . I'll tell you everything; but not now.' Her personality seemed to have changed, the experience leaving its mark, making her gentle instead of aggressive. The physical ordeal had given her an almost pathetic frailty. The wedding had automatically been postponed.

It was a week after returning home that she said to Janet, 'I want to have a quiet little dinner with you, Ross, Anita and Kenneth—to celebrate, if you like, my being dragged back to life. There are things I want to say . . . I'm perfectly all right now,' she insisted.

And as Anita dressed for that evening, she thought how ironic it was that Glynis's near-suicide had forced her into a position where she could not avoid meeting Ross socially, and without antagonism.

Kenneth called for her, his dismay at all that had happened, matching her own. The mystery remained, and to Anita the suspense was unbearable since she dreaded the inevitable moment when Ross was revealed as the lover of a ward he was supposed to protect. Glynis looked calm as she greeted them, kissing Anita with warmth, her gratitude genuine. Nevertheless there was an air of unreality about her as though she found life a poignant struggle, and communication an effort

It was after dinner and over coffee, that she said as the tension mounted, 'I suppose what I'm going to say ought to be just for Ross's ears only, but I think it will be easier if I include you all, since you'll have to be told. It isn't going to be easy, so please bear with me.' She looked at Ross intently, 'You have a right to know why I intended to kill myself.'

Anita shivered as she saw Ross start, his expression anxious. Now he would have the humiliation of hearing the truth broadcast and she suffered for him.

He exclaimed, 'Glynis, please don't distress yourself. Wait until you are stronger.'

'No; I can't keep the secret any longer, *bear* it . . .' The words rushed out, almost on the edge of hysteria, 'I'm going to have a child, and you know,

Ross, it couldn't be yours because we've never been lovers.'

The immediate silence was heavy with shock and disbelief.

Ross's voice held stunned incredulity, as he echoed, 'A *child*; but—'

Anita sat there, hearing Glynis's words with a terrible sensation of guilt and regret as she realised how badly she had misjudged him.

Glynis, pale, shaking, seemed to shrink back into her chair, as though seeking its sanctuary, as she went on, calmer now, 'I couldn't go through with the deception when it came to it. I intended marrying you and not saying anything. Premature babies are born every day. And when one is desperate, one thinks of the most dreadful and fantastic things to avoid disaster and being found out.'

They sat, stupefied, hearing, hardly believing, each making a little gesture, but without speaking.

Ross was momentarily speechless before he protested, 'But you must have known the truth would be discovered in the end.'

She shook her head and sighed deeply.

'I refused to face facts until the other night. I argued that medical people are notoriously blind when it comes to the ills of those close to them and that, anyway, you trusted me implicitly, so that it wouldn't enter your head that the child was not yours. It was a calculated risk that I was prepared to take because it overcame an immediate crisis.' She lowered her head in a little humble gesture, before looking him in the face. 'I had always intended to marry you,' she admitted with a touch of her old complacency.

'My God!' Ross cried. 'So that was why *you* suggested marriage, and wanted to rush things.'

'And *your* words, "The sooner the better",' she reminded him.

The silence built up into suspense and unease, and they watched Glynis, half-fascinated by what seemed a pitiful strength in the circumstances. Her voice grew stronger as she went on, 'I've learned a great deal in these past few days; seen myself as I really am, and knew that I could not go on pretending even if the deception could have worked. Panic made me take the tablets; panic and a terrible fear that came over me like a madness, if you like. I couldn't see any way out. The enormity of it just made something snap. Also, I was miserable about you,' she added deliberately, 'but that's another story.'

Janet said painfully, compassionately, 'but surely you could have told *me*?'

Glynis looked at her and tears came. 'Oh, yes; I could have told you, dear Janet, and put the burden on your shoulders, because Ross was involved.'

And suddenly, Ross's voice thundered into the silence. 'And the man? Who is the man—the father?'

Glynis shook her head. 'He's not important. Someone I met and was madly attracted to—physically. There was no question of my marrying him. And no point in our discussing him.'

Ross made an impatient gesture. 'I still want to know his name.' He spoke with authority, his expression grim and determined.

Again there was a dangerous silence during which Glynis's resolve hardened, and she shook her head. 'I'm sorry. I cannot tell you.'

And suddenly, dramatically, Kenneth said, 'I know his name.'

Glynis cried appealingly, 'No; *no*. It won't help, or do any good.'

But Kenneth ignored her as he said quietly, 'I know, because *I* am the man; but God help me, I didn't know there was to be a child.'

All Glynis's control vanished when she saw the stunned, appalled look on Ross's face as he sat there, too shocked to speak. Great sobs tore at her as Kenneth exclaimed, 'Why didn't you tell me. Why?'

'Because you didn't love me; you love Anita, so what good would my telling you have done?'

Ross stared at Kenneth as he murmured disbelievingly, 'You and Glynis! *You!*' His voice was hollow and empty.

Kenneth didn't lower his gaze as he said, 'I don't expect you to understand. The attraction between us was overwhelming. I'm not arguing the rights or wrongs of the case. It wasn't until Anita came back into the picture and I realised I loved her—'

Glynis interrupted, looking at Anita shamefaced, 'I used you; built up your friendship with Kenneth so that Ross would suspect you were lovers. I was jealous, both because of Kenneth *and* Ross. And I wanted to divert attention from Kenneth and me. I know I was often horrid to you.' She turned to Ross. 'Please don't hate me too much. Emotion can be so shattering, so terrible. I wanted to be *loved*.' She paused, catching her breath, 'You have always loved me as a ward—protectively, and with devotion. You have never been *in* love with

me, or given me cause to think you were. I made
Janet believe that you and I would eventually be
married, in order to conceal my relationship with
Kenneth, and because I knew that if anyone would
suspect, she would. Also, I've always wanted to
marry you, because I like the life you have given
me, as well as everything you stand for; but, then,
when it came to it, I knew that even if I were your
wife, I'd still have nothing, because you didn't love
me either, and material things wouldn't have com-
pensated. In addition I should have wrecked your
whole future . . . Oh, Ross; please forgive me;
forgive me.' Tears rolled down her cheeks. 'I was so
desperate; so desolate. There was no one, and I
was a coward about the baby. You were my only
salvation. Kenneth was a wild infatuation, a physical attraction—' She seemed to crumple in her chair.
'I couldn't bear to lose your friendship—' The
words were stifled, her voice breaking.

Ross got up and stood, back to the chimney-
piece. There was a grimness about him, disillusionment and anger mounting as he thought of Glynis's
scheming against Anita; the lies that had deceived
them all. But he knew that this was not the moment
to enlarge upon it; the problem went too deep. Her
relationship with Kenneth was a different matter
and he said gravely, 'Who am I to sit in judgment?
Nothing in life is either black or white, and who
among us has escaped being at the mercy of
emotion?'

Glynis stumbled across the room and flung herself into his arms. 'Now nothing else matters,' she
cried. '*Nothing.*'

Anita sat there, forgiving, and near breaking

point. It was impossible for the truth to sink in. *Kenneth* of all people. Yet ought she not to have guessed? How often had he criticised himself emotionally; been ill at ease, like a man guarding a secret? And Ross! The memory of all she had said to him seered her. And now his words, 'Who am I to sit in judgment?', increased his stature and eradicated all hint of hypocrisy.

Glynis, controlled now, returned to her chair, addressing Ross as she said quietly, 'I don't want any loose ends—anything that can leave doubt or suspicion. I've gone over every point since I came out of hospital, and I realise that if you had not been so indifferent about your own happiness, and your life generally, you would never have agreed to marry me, or accepted the idea so lightly; neither would you have allowed *me* to plan the future, and have more or less a secret marriage.'

Ross didn't speak; he remained standing, his calm impressive.

Glynis went on, 'You were like a sleep-walker going through the motions of being a fiancé—never actually *being* one. At the time it didn't matter, because all I thought about was myself and, as I have already said, I had always schemed, in my own fashion, to marry you, irrespective of my relationship with Kenneth. I would like to think that one day I can love someone more than I love myself . . . but now you are free.'

Ross could not mouth platitudes, and his silence was more eloquent than words. It also established the truth of Glynis' summing up.

Janet murmured, 'How little we know about each other; and how much we have to learn.'

Kenneth spoke up, this time with authority, looking at Glynis, 'Since this is a moment when honesty is its one redeeming feature, I want the child, Glynis. You will marry me,' he added forcefully, 'and we won't pretend.'

'Marry you?' Her eyes widened, but a glimmer of hope flashed across her face.

Ross made no gesture of protest.

'Yes,' Kenneth insisted. 'Who knows, we may find happiness and win back a little respect. We are two free people, and I believe a child is better off with two parents.' He looked at Anita with a lingering tenderness and, in that look, said goodbye.

Ross studied Glynis with a mixture of compassion and concern, without losing sight of her injustice to Anita, but his voice was strong and supportive as he said, 'You don't have to make any decisions on social grounds. Janet and I are here, and all that has happened makes no difference to our relationship. If you marry Kenneth, then we'll start again and put all this behind us.'

Glynis moved to the sofa and sat down beside Kenneth. It was a gesture of solidarity.

'*I* think a child needs its father,' she said quietly. 'And I wouldn't like to be on my own. No pretence,' she said, and her voice grew stronger.

Ross met Kenneth's gaze, and the memory of years of friendship lay between them.

'I will take care of her,' Kenneth said simply.

Ross didn't hesitate. 'I believe you,' he replied.

Glynis said, as she turned to Anita, 'Try to forgive me; I'm so sorry and ashamed . . . you've been so good to me, too,' she added. 'You knew I was pregnant, and have kept my secret.' Her gaze flashed to Ross, 'That morning at the pool—'

'What?' he exclaimed, his voice sharp, critical. In the look he exchanged with Anita were the words, 'So you naturally thought the child was mine.' There was an appalled expression of distaste in his eyes.

Glynis pleaded, 'Perhaps you could persuade Anita to come back to Harley Street.' There was a deep significance in the words.

Ross broke the tense silence by saying, 'I'd like to talk to Anita.'

Janet got up from her chair. She didn't speak but, on the way out, put her hand on Anita's in a little understanding gesture. Kenneth and Glynis followed solemnly.

Anita felt sick with emotion as the door shut and she and Ross were alone. There was so much to say, to explain, and for which to apologise. But as she looked up at him, the same yearning, attraction, desire, flooded over her so that she cried involuntarily, 'Oh, Ross; I'm so *sorry* for all I said that afternoon. So desperately sorry. It was unforgivable.'

'Not when you allow for all you had been led to believe.'

'It was Janet who told me that your engagement was going to be announced at any time, and coming from her there was no room for doubt.'

His voice was strong and demanding, 'Was there love in your anger and contempt? Did you hate me so much for what you believed to be my defection, that you fell in love with me, too?'

Anita felt a wild excitement engulfing her as she cried, 'Yes . . . it was only then that I *realised*.'

He stood there triumphant and challenging. 'Say it, Anita,' he whispered.

'I love you, Ross.'

He reached out and drew her into his arms as though defying the world to part them, his kiss thrilling, almost stifling.

'It's been sheer hell,' he admitted. 'Hell.' His eyes looked deeply into hers. 'I love you,' he said passionately. 'At first I didn't believe it, but I was merely deceiving myself. There was *love* in my wanting you,' he added gently, and with tenderness. 'Believe that, my darling.'

'I do,' she said, 'but oh, Ross; I was furious, jealous, afraid—just everything a woman can be, when I thought of you with Glynis—'

'You had every justification,' he said grimly. 'Don't imagine that I can overlook her part in all this.'

'She has suffered enough,' Anita murmured. 'There's no deception in her remorse.'

'I was a fool,' he admitted, with a gesture of disgust, 'not to see that my relationship with her was open to conjecture. Men are arrogant, thoughtless creatures. And I was so damned jealous of Kenneth.'

'I not only had Glynis to be jealous of, but Fleur Sheriden, too,' she added.

'Fleur!' He looked astounded. 'But she is just a friendly patient who needs my help on occasion.' It went through Ross's mind that Glynis might have built up the relationship.

'Oh,' Anita exclaimed, relieved and a little apologetic, and in that second a flash of memory thrilled her anew, as she thought of Ross, her former employer—inscrutable, magnetic, and of whom she had once almost stood in awe. Now, here she was *with* him, misunderstandings at an end.

'And you do understand why I allowed myself to become engaged to Glynis?' He spoke urgently. 'After that scene with you, nothing mattered. I was shattered, and could see no hope for the future.'

'I understand,' she assured him.

'I love you,' he repeated almost solemnly, 'and I have never uttered those words to any other woman,' he added, as he drew her back into his arms. 'Will you marry me, my darling?'

Her kiss was his answer.

Doctor Nurse Romances